Even when your strength was gone, even when you could barely form a clear thought, if you hated somebody enough, you found sudden, overwhelming strength.

Fargo hurled himself at a stunned Farraday, smashing fists into his face, his throat, his chest, his sternum, and his belly before Farraday could raise a single hand in response. His two cronies shouted oaths and curses. One of them took his gun out. But he sure as hell couldn't shoot into this blur of flying fists and tumbling bodies without endangering Farraday's life. He put his pistol back in the holster. And neither man wanted to get tangled up in the brawl.

This Fargo—who just a minute ago had looked so pale and exhausted that he could barely stand up— he'd turned into some kind of murderous whirling dervish. If he wasn't pounding on Farraday, he was kicking him; if he wasn't kicking him, he was head-butting him. He seemed crazed, like a man who had suddenly lost all sense and reason and was some kind of animal that could be brought down only by a fusillade of gunfire.

THE
TRAILSMAN
#270

COLORADO
CORPSE

by

Jon Sharpe

A SIGNET BOOK

SIGNET
Published by New American Library, a division of
Penguin Group (USA) Inc., 375 Hudson Street,
New York, New York 10014, U.S.A.
Penguin Books Ltd, 80 Strand,
London WC2R 0RL, England
Penguin Books Australia Ltd, 250 Camberwell Road,
Camberwell, Victoria 3124, Australia
Penguin Books Canada Ltd, 10 Alcorn Avenue,
Toronto, Ontario, Canada M4V 3B2
Penguin Books (N.Z.) Ltd, Cnr Rosedale and Airborne Roads,
Albany, Auckland 1310, New Zealand

Penguin Books Ltd, Registered Offices:
80 Strand, London WC2R 0RL, England

First published by Signet, an imprint of New American Library,
a division of Penguin Group (USA) Inc.

First Printing, April 2004
10 9 8 7 6 5 4 3 2 1

The first chapter of this book originally appeared in *Devil's Den*, the two
hundred sixty-ninth volume in this series.

Copyright © Penguin Group (USA) Inc., 2004
All rights reserved

 REGISTERED TRADEMARK—MARCA REGISTRADA

Printed in the United States of America

PUBLISHER'S NOTE
This is a work of fiction. Names, characters, places, and incidents either are
the product of the author's imagination or are used fictitiously, and any resem-
blance to actual persons, living or dead, business establishments, events, or
locales is entirely coincidental.

The Trailsman

Beginnings . . . they bend the tree and they mark the man. Skye Fargo was born when he was eighteen. Terror was his midwife, vengeance his first cry. Killing spawned Skye Fargo, ruthless, cold-blooded murder. Out of the acrid smoke of gunpowder still hanging in the air, he rose, cried out a promise never forgotten.

The Trailsman they began to call him all across the West: searcher, scout, hunter, the man who could see where others only looked, his skills for hire but not his soul, the man who lived each day to the fullest, yet trailed each tomorrow. Skye Fargo, the Trailsman, the seeker who could take the wildness of a land and the wanting of a woman and make them his own.

Colorado Territory, 1862—
The beauty of the land,
the ugliness of lawlessness and murder.

1

Odd. The door to a fancy hotel suite standing half-open like this.

And not a single sound coming from inside.

Skye Fargo stood in the second-floor hallway of the exclusive Mountain View hotel, which was a gilded tribute to the good luck of the locals. While a lot of Colorado boomtowns had gone bust in the past ten years, Mountain View had turned into a prosperous and permanent town thanks to the rich veins of gold-streaked quartz in the surrounding mountains.

This hotel, with its carpeted hall and brocaded wallpaper and elegant French sconces, was a tribute to the good fortune the locals had enjoyed for eight years now. The saloon and dining facilities on the main floor were even more imposing.

Fargo drew his Colt. That probably wasn't the polite thing to do in a place as refined as this, but he didn't care. He sensed something wrong. And he'd survived by trusting his senses.

In addition to the door being half-open and only silence coming from inside, the suite was dark. The only illumination was from the street lamps below.

It was near midnight, the time at which he was supposed to meet the mysterious Carlotta Massett, the woman who'd left a note for him saying that she could help keep his friend Curt Cates from hanging for mur-

1

der three days from now. She claimed she knew the identity of the real killer and asked that he meet her in her suite at midnight.

He inched the door inward. Stepped across the threshold.

"Carlotta?" he said, his voice sounding ghostlike in the silence. "Carlotta?"

He stood in the center of the large parlor that was filled with a fireplace, two huge couches, and other furnishings in the heavily decorous Renaissance Revival style, the British style preferred by the wealthy Americans.

A mewing sound came from near his feet. He looked down to see a tiny kitten, one so small it looked as if it could fit into his large palm, craning its neck upward to see the giant hovering above it. The kitten's fur was mostly white except for a few mixed patches of brown and black. It was too dark to see any other detail.

"Hey there, little one," he said. "Where's your mistress?"

The kitten just mewed again.

Fargo decided to look into the bedroom. He expected to find it empty. No way she would've gone to sleep after leaving him that note.

He walked wide of the feline, not wanting to crush her with one of his boots.

The killer had been hiding at the far end of the second floor, in the closet where the maids stored their buckets and mops and dusters.

The killer watched as Fargo entered the room number that had been printed on the note the killer had sent Fargo this afternoon. The note signed as "Carlotta Massett." Whoever the hell that was.

Now the second part of the evening's work would have to get under way. This might prove to be difficult. Many were the tales told of the Trailsman, and if even

2

half of them were true, he was no man to take chances with.

But the deed must be done and done now. No telling how long Fargo would be in the hotel suite before deciding that he'd been duped. And leave.

The killer moved swiftly, surely.

Neither lamplight nor moonlight pressed against the bedroom drapes. The room was cave-dark. The interior of the canopied bed was almost ominous in its black depths.

Fargo found a lantern. He scraped a lucifer against his belt buckle and got the lantern going. Shimmering gold light filled the room with wavering illumination.

More money had been spent on decorating this bed-chamber than any twenty men earned in a year. The armoires were expansive enough to need double doors. He threw them open, held the lantern inside.

Empty.

Strange. A woman who could afford a suite like this not having at least a few clothes hanging in the closet.

The empty armoires reminded him that he'd seen nothing personal at all in this suite. As if nobody was staying in it. As if the hotel maid had just finished getting it ready between guests.

He searched the rest of the room, finding no trace of anybody who might be staying here. He'd been skeptical of the note—it could easily have been a trap—and now he wondered if he'd been stupid to come here in the first place.

He wanted to find the real killer so that his friend wouldn't die. But the real killer obviously didn't want to be found. Had it been the real killer who'd sent the note?

As he started to lift his boot, he felt a slight pressure on the arch of his left foot. The kitten. He set the lantern down on the elaborately carved bureau with its gigantic oval mirror. Then he bent down and picked up the kitten, stroking her head to satisfy her lonely need.

In the lantern light, he saw that the white fur on her left side was spattered with something liquid and dark. He held her closer to the lantern.

No mistaking what it was. Fargo surveyed the chamber. He'd sure missed something important in his search.

The canopy bed. After taking a second inventory of the room with a few quick glances, he realized what he'd overlooked. The canopy bed—underneath. The fancy burgundy-colored bedspread reached the floor. The kitten had crawled beneath it and gone exploring.

Now it was Fargo's turn to go exploring.

He walked to the bed, got down on his knees, and lifted up the bedspread.

He needed a few seconds for his eyes to adjust to the darkness but soon enough he saw where the kitten had picked up the blood. The naked body of a once lovely, now dead, woman faced him. Her eyes had grown enormous in the last horrible moments of her life. Her open mouth shaped a silent scream.

He got up and went to the bureau, got the lantern and brought it back. He wanted a better look at the woman and the situation under the bed.

The sweet-faced but blood-spattered kitten pranced proudly behind him. Whether Fargo liked it or not, he'd made a new friend.

Now that he could see the corpse better, he saw that the killer had beaten her up before killing her. A kerchief lay nearby. He'd probably gagged her so nobody could hear her scream.

He thought he heard something but when he glanced up, he saw nothing. He couldn't see much,

4

anyway. The chamber was three-quarters dark again with the lantern down on the floor.

The kitten sat about a foot from his hand, watching alertly.

He thought about dragging the woman out from under the bed but realized that was unwise. He'd go for the law and show her to them just as he'd found her. He'd kept the note, too. He'd also show them that. Though he'd been here for a time, he hadn't met the sheriff or any of the deputies. His friend said they were bad people who held the town captive. But you couldn't expect a man who was about to hang to have much good to say about the people who wanted to hang him, could you?

The kitten jumped at him suddenly, meaning to be friendly and playful, but knocked over the lantern instead. Fire was the constant enemy of hotels. The lantern spilled some fuel immediately.

Fargo moved quickly. He righted the lantern and felt along the dark stain on the floor. He'd get some water and wash it off.

That was when it happened.

If Fargo hadn't been busy with the kitten, the lantern, and the spilled fuel, he would have heard the footsteps before it was too late.

He would have jerked away from the descending arc of the heavy fireplace poker. . . .

And then he would have jumped to his feet and hurled himself at the person who'd just crept into the room.

But preoccupied as he was with a room literally crawling with distractions, his response was too little and too late. The poker was swung with such force that his instincts for self-preservation were frozen even before they could reach his consciousness.

The wound was so savage and so deep that his blood was splashed against the wall in dark, sticky

5

pieces so heavy and hairy they did not resemble anything that could have come from a human being.

When the killer was sure that Fargo was unconscious, the rest of the work was undertaken. Fast work, accurate work, important work.

2

A woman's work was never done. . . .

For Serena Cates it had been a day of washing clothes down at the creek, baking bread, cutting her three-year-old son Tommy's hair, grooming the family horse, darning socks, sweeping out the barn, rushing to a false alarm at which she would have been mid-wife, putting up preserves, and then going into town to buy a few candles and . . .

. . . and seeing her husband Curt in jail.

Her father, a farmer, used to say: "We ain't got much, honeygirl. But at least we got our reputation. Not a one of us ever been in jail."

Serena knew that she had a nice body and so did the deputy, Andy Madden, who always appraised her up and down with a stupid leer on his wide, mean face.

"I'd like to see my husband."

"And he'd be a fool not to see you." He managed to drag his boots down off the desk and sit up in his chair and splay both his hands over his knees. He made everything look like a big effort. "I had a gal like you at home, I'd never make it into work." There were some who didn't like Serena. She'd been married before Curt to a man who'd died mighty young and mysterious. She was seen as a hussy, of course, by the primmest of the town's women.

"Please," she said. "I don't like to hear talk like that."

He stood up, lean, leathery. "Oh, that's right. You're a church-goin' lady, aren't you? Maybe your husband shoulda gone with you more often. Maybe then he wouldn't have run around with whores and ended up killin' one."

She didn't want to please him by getting angry or acting hurt. She said, coldly, "Sheriff Burrell told me I could see Curt any time I wanted to during the day."

The deputy shrugged. "Sure wouldn't want to go against Henry's word, now, would I?"

He dragged himself over to the wall where the jail keys hung on a peg. "Smells're pretty bad today. Colored man who cleans everything up around here had to go to a funeral. And we had four drunks back there last night." He turned to face her, holding the keys up as if they were some sort of prize. "Fact, the night deputy, he had to put one of 'em in the cell with your husband." He winked. "I guess ole Curt is more of a lover than a fighter, huh?"

Her stomach knotted. Curt *wasn't* much of a fighter. That was one of the things that had drawn her to him when they were teenagers. Where the other boys always used violence to settle their disputes, Curt used common sense. He was more likely to break up fights than to get in them. The same for being true. Where other boys took to saloons as soon as they reached the proper age, Curt hated the places because they'd killed his father, who'd been both a drinker and a brawler, dying one night when another drunk smashed a whiskey bottle over his head, killing him instantly. And the idea that Curt would be seeing a teenage girl . . .

But that was the charge that held him here in prison. That he'd gotten involved with a teenage girl who lived about a mile away. And then, when she threatened to tell her folks, he'd killed her. Two witnesses claimed to have seen Curt and Lilly Potter sneaking off into the woods several times. One even claimed to have seen them making love. The jury had stayed out a grand total of eighteen minutes before returning a verdict of guilty. And the judge pronounced sentence on the spot: death by hanging. . . .

The odors gagged her as soon as Andy Madden jerked open the heavy, timbered door leading to the four cells in back. Vomit. Urine. Blood.

The drunks had apparently been released. The only prisoner in the place lay on his back, his forearm covering his face. She'd need to bring Curt some fresh clothes. He'd worn the gray work shirt and faded butternuts for a week now.

Curt obviously heard her, took his arm away, sat up.

Her gasp was sharp as a gunshot in the filthy silence of the jail.

Most of his face on the left side was a series of inter-connected bruises. His right eye was grotesquely swollen and the color of a grape. His lips were cracked and caked with dried blood.

"Somebody should be protecting him," she snapped at the deputy.

"I guess the night man must've gotten busy with other stuff, huh? Isn't that about right, Curt?"

Her husband was a slender but sinewy man, already losing his hair at twenty-three. He had a glare that could pierce rock. He visited it on Madden now. Madden just sneered and shook his head.

"Looks like he needs his mama," he said to Serena. "I better get outta here before he starts cryin'."

"You forgot to open the cell door," she said.

He grinned and let his eyes roam her chest. "Guess I musta got distracted."

He let her in and locked up.

"You ain't able to handle her, Cates, I'll be happy to pitch in for ya."

Curt jerked up from the floor cot he'd been lying

on but Serena put a hand on his arm. Curt didn't need to get hit again, something Madden would be only too happy to do.

When he was gone, she said, "I'll send Doc Hastings over here."

"I'll be all right."

"But somebody beat you very bad, honey."

He looked at her and smiled. "Yeah, but you should've seen what *he* looked like when they took him out of here this morning."

She returned his smile. "Yes, I'll bet you just pulverized him, didn't you?"

"Actually, I caught him a couple of good ones right on the jaw. That was the only thing that saved me, hitting him hard as I could. Otherwise he would've kept on pounding me."

He showed her his bruised knuckles. She saw a kind of pride in his blue eyes she'd never seen before. He'd graduated last night into the fraternity of fighters. Mild as his temperament was, it was a fraternity he obviously was proud to be a member of. "And that made me think of a couple of other fellas I might look up when I get out of here." Then it obviously all came back to him. The arrest. The jail. The inquest. The trial. The verdict. The death sentence. "*If* I ever get out of here."

She took his hand, careful not to hold it too tightly. The knuckles were as bruised as his face. "You'll get out of here. You know how Fargo is. He won't quit until he finds the real killer."

They'd met Fargo a few years back when he was being chased by a band of Indians. He'd stopped them from torturing one of their own braves who'd done something to profoundly piss off the chief. Whatever his offense, the brave—still clearly in his teens—didn't deserve to have his skin flayed with a whip with a razor-sharp arrowhead mounted on its tip. Fargo had

10

been badly wounded by an arrow to his shoulder. A mortal infection was setting in.

He collapsed near a clearing that Curt Cates was making alone with his ax and his strong back and his pure, simple pioneer grit.

Curt found him and brought him home. When the Indians came, he and Serena hid him in the tiny root cellar. It took nearly twenty-four hours for the fever to break. And another twenty-four before Fargo was anything like coherent. The Indians snuck back later but Curt had heard them approach and snuck Fargo back to the root cellar.

Fargo wouldn't be alive today if he hadn't had their help. And he acknowledged the debt by stopping by the homestead a few days previous, wanting to give them some of the money he'd earned as a reward for killing a particularly murderous bank robber. That's when he learned about Curt's murder charge and death sentence. There were a lot of men who might go off track—who might pick up with a girl and start sexing her on the side; and a lot of men who might get scared when she threatened to tell her parents about the relationship—but he knew with total certainty that Curt Cates wasn't among their number.

Fargo went into town and paid off all their bills at various stores. And then he appointed himself to the job of finding out who really killed the girl.

"He told me that somebody had written him a note," she said, telling her husband about her last conversation with Fargo. "He was supposed to meet her in a hotel suite at midnight last night."

"No word from him since?"

"No."

"That's pretty strange—some woman meeting him in a hotel room. If she's from out of town, how would she know anything about the murder?"

"I thought it was strange, too—and so did Fargo.

But he said that was the only real lead he'd gotten in two days."

He sighed and then took her in his arms. "I hope he can find something out. There isn't much time left."

No, she thought. No, there isn't much time left. She fought off tears, not so much for her sake as for his. He had all the grief he could handle.

Five minutes after the Cates woman left, his erection gone with her, Deputy Andy Madden was sitting behind his desk when the front door opened and the sheriff's son Hap came in. A lot of people didn't like Hap because he was so handsome he was almost pretty; and a lot of other people didn't like him because his old man let him get away with things he'd jail other twenty-year-olds for; and still others didn't like him because he couldn't hold a job, snuck around with the wives of other men, and was strongly suspected of sticking up a few businesses. Seems like the sheriff, so competent in other ways, just never could figure out who'd robbed certain places.

Hap said, "You got my money, Andy?"

As usual, Hap was dressed in city clothes, dress shirt and trousers, fancy white low-brimmed hat. He carried what was called a six-shooter in his holster, which was tied down gunny-style. Nobody had ever tested Hap—so-named because of that smile the gals liked so much, his real name being Eugene—because they were afraid that he might just be as fast as he pretended to be. Not to mention that even if they did kill him, they figured his old man would run them in for murder.

Madden didn't hide his displeasure. What he wanted to say was that he—and everybody else at the table three nights ago—knew damned well that Hap had been dealing off the bottom of the deck. He never resorted to cheating unless he was losing badly. And then—watch out. He'd taken a good deal of Madden's money. In one sense, Madden had only himself to blame—or at least that was what his wife would say if she ever found out—here he knew he was being cheated but he didn't stop playing. Hap (his wife would go on) had *forced* him to play, hadn't he? All that might be true. But the fact remained that Hap cheated.

Madden was almost ready to make the accusation every poker player in town was almost ready to make—*You're a damned cardsharp, Hap*—but now he forced himself to be silent. Hap had him in a bind. You go around accusing the sheriff's son of being a cardsharp—you can kiss your ass and your deputy's badge good-bye.

Hap smirked. "Pop always pays you boys right at the end of your shift. Just wanted to let you know I'll be here. You know, in case you'd be thinkin' of sneakin' off without me gettin' my fair share of your wages."

As always when he told people things they didn't want to hear, Hap kept his hand set just so on the handle of his gun.

That made his silent message loud and clear.

He gave a jaunty little salute off the brim of his fancy white hat and left.

The large man in buckskins had had some pretty bad hangovers in his time but not a single one approached this one. His head throbbed so badly that he was afraid to open his eyes. He also felt a peculiar weakness in his extremities.

And then he realized something odd. It did not panic him, not at first. He simply accepted the reality of it.

He couldn't remember who he was.

He knew about hangovers. He knew about feeling weak. And when he managed to wrestle one eyelid open, he knew that he was in a room with a fancy wallpapered ceiling.

13

He knew all the things a normal human being would. And he did all the normal things a human being would. He scratched. He yawned—even though that made the pounding headache even worse—and he tried to raise himself up from the floor.

But he couldn't remember who he was.

All human beings had names. Dogs and parrots and ships and mountains and rivers had names.

But what was his name?

Rising from the floor seemed to take several days. He'd start to sit up but the headache would be so bad that he'd have to tenderly lay himself back down. Then he'd try again. On what felt like the three thousandth attempt, he managed to sit up and look around.

He'd never seen this room before.

Canopied bed. Flocked wallpaper. Persian carpets. Heavy, expensive, British furniture.

Then he thought: how do I know it's British furniture? If I don't know who I am, how the hell can I tell British furniture from American furniture?

And then a terrifying flood of other questions: How did I get here? And what happened to my head? And how long have I been here? And what's that terrible stench? And what's all over my hands?

Last question first: what was all over his hands?

Even in his confused and weakened state, he knew the answer to that one. He just didn't want to acknowledge the answer was all.

Because it was pretty obvious what was all over his hands, all over his shirt, all over his pants. Blood.

And then a strange, tiny sound, one that took a moment to register.

A kitten appeared.

A pert little white thing, its scruffy beauty marred by the same liquid that had dried on his hands. Blood. The kitten somehow figured in this, too.

The kitten crawled up in his lap. He stroked it with

his bloody hand, grateful to feel the warm pulsing life of the tiny creature. Its damp pink nose was almost comical.

And then he saw the upturned hand that lay just under the edge of the fancy canopied bed. A female hand, slight, very pretty, actually, except for the deep ugly gashes across the palm.

He knew then where the stench was coming from.

He didn't know his name—didn't have a clue about his identity—but by God he knew a corpse when he saw one. A hand twisted at that particular angle, and slashed the way it was—that was not the hand of a living person.

But how did he know about corpses?

Was he a violent man, used to being around the slain and defiled?

And then, of course, the inevitable question, the most damning question of all: had he killed this woman?

If he didn't know his name, if he didn't know his identity, then he couldn't know his nature. Was he the kind of man capable of such a thing?

The kitten jumped down and walked over to something nearby. The man had to angle his head to see it, angle it in such a way that it only increased the pounding pain in his head.

A knife. The kind a man might carry in a scabbard on his belt. The knife blade was as bloody as the man's hand.

The kitten feinted at it with its tiny paw but then drew back. Apparently, it didn't want any more blood on its mostly white body.

The thought was simple enough when it came to him: *get out of here*. No matter who you are, no matter what you did, you need to get out of here. Now.

But his body—whoever he was—would not cooperate with his instincts. When he leaned forward to peer

15

under the bed, he got so dizzy he collapsed face down. It took him a couple of minutes before he was able to open his eyes again.

He got his first real look at her.

She'd been a beauty. Past tense. Even in the shadows beneath the bed, even slashed and gouged and bloody, something of her elegant presence was still there.

He had the same questions for her as he had for himself. Who was she? Why was she in this room? What was her name? Where was she from?

But these questions only begged the more serious one: had he killed her? And if so, why? Had he loved her, only to learn that she'd betrayed him? Had they been partners in some scheme and he'd found out that she'd cheated him? Or—hopefully—had someone else killed her? But if so, why was he stained with her blood? And was the nearby knife his own?

Questions without answers.

Once again, he tried to stand up. Needed to get out of here. Now.

He made it. Took four attempts. Took sweat, swearing, panic, and a strength he hadn't been sure he was capable of. But he managed to get to his feet and turn toward the door leading out of the chamber where—

—where the maid stood.

She was a squat, white woman in a dress of faded gingham. She had the bright blue accusing eyes of the neighborhood gossip. Malice gleamed in those eyes. She was probably in her thirties.

She looked at him, at the blood, and said, "Are you all right, sir?"

"I—I fell out of bed last night and hurt myself."

Her smile was as callous as her gaze. "That must've been quite a fall, sir, to draw so much blood." Then her eyes found the knife on the floor. Her entire body and face tightened. She was coming to conclusions—

and probably correct ones—that could do him no good at all.

She said, "I'll come back later, when you're feeling better."

She wants out of here. She's afraid. She'll go down to the desk clerk. Send somebody for the law. The blood all over me. The knife. They'll find the dead woman right away. The law. A posse . . . I need to clear my head. Something is . . . wrong with me.

The maid began to back slowly out of the room. As if he were a crazed animal who would attack her if she made any sudden movement.

"Listen—wait—I—"

He started toward her.

She drew back, eyes searching to make sure she had a clear passage to the hallway and to safety.

"I need to explain myself—"

"No need to explain to me, sir." Her voice trembled. Her cheeks were pale. Her eyes—once so judgmental and dismissive—were now frantic.

"That isn't my knife on the floor there—"

"Whatever you say, sir. I just need to get on with my work. Mornings are my busy time." Voice shaking even harder now.

The thought came to him that maybe he *should* grab her. *Should* tie her up and gag her so that he had time to get away.

Need to clear my head, so confused . . . can't think . . . can't remember.

Then she was gone.

He couldn't have moved quickly enough even if he'd wanted to. For somebody as heavyset as she was, she'd moved with terrific speed and purpose.

Gone.

How long would it be before this hotel suite was filled with lawmen with guns? How long would it be before they'd accuse him of murdering the woman under the bed? How long would it be before he'd see his life drawing to a close as the hangman's knot swung idly in the breeze, waiting for a masked executioner to lead him up the steps to the gallows?

Need to clear my head, so confused . . .

What choice did he have? He did the only thing he could. He walked over to the bedroom window. There was a wooden fire escape built onto the rear wall.

He pushed the window up.

If only he didn't have blood all over. Maybe he could pass himself off as just another stranger—if he was a stranger in this town. But with all the blood . . .

But there wasn't time to worry about that now.

He climbed out to the fire escape.

The day hit him. Sunlight. Jingle and jangle and jostle of the main street that ran in front of the hotel. He felt alien, as if he didn't belong in this world or among these people. Normal people. He was some other kind of being, a hurting, sweaty, angry, scared specimen that was not of the human race. A specimen with no memory of who he was, what he was about, what he'd done.

He did the only thing he could. He ran.

3

Sheriff Henry Burrell was liked because he was different from most lawmen. To the citizens he served, he was generally polite, soft-spoken, helpful. He had a temper but usually kept it in check. He was, like most lawmen, beholden to the elite group that had hired him, but he tried to give most people a decent break. He was slight, bald, and carried with him a certain melancholy. His wife had died some time back, leaving him with a son whom she'd spoiled so badly that he got into trouble just about every week, leaving his humiliated father to bail him out—literally.

He was finishing his breakfast at the café when Slocum burst through the front door of the place and hurried over to him. Slocum loved a fuss. Three times a week at a minimum he'd coming wailing up to Burrell to report some terrible, town-threatening deed that had gone on at the fancy hotel he managed. Most of his urgent reports had to do with guests he suspected of "foul deeds." If a week went by when Slocum didn't happen upon foreign spies, international jewel thieves, or gunrunners who sold to Indians, it wasn't a week worth living.

"This is a bad one, Sheriff," Slocum said, breathless, his pig-face blood red and glazed with sweat.

"Usually is, Donald," Burrell said around a piece of flank steak. Slocum was one of the few people he was mean to. Donald doted on the misery of others.

"I'm serious." Gasping still from his run.

Burrell sawed off a piece of flapjack—which was every bit as tough as the flank steak—and brought it to his mouth.

"You hear what I said, Sheriff? I said this is a bad one."

"I heard, Donald."

The morning crowd enjoyed it when Slocum came in like this and the sheriff treated him with such amiable contempt. The two put on a show, sort of like Punch and Judy. The onlookers would smirk, giggle, point, nod, and in general have about as good a time as you could have and still be legal. Except for a new batch of prostitutes, making fun of people was about the only good time you could have in a town like this.

"Donald, why don't you get yourself a cup of coffee and go over there to that empty table and sit down and wait till I get done eating?"

"But Sheriff—"

"Digestion, Donald," Burrell said. "A man don't digest right, it gives him gas and it gives him stomach burn. Now you don't want me to have gas and stomach burn, do you?"

This was one of the best shows Punch and Judy had ever put on. The sheriff had never banished him to a table before. This was great.

"But Sheriff, please, listen. I—"

"Donald," Burrell said, using his fork to point at the empty chair across the way. "Go over there and sit down. We'll talk in a few minutes." The lawman pointed the tines of his fork at the other part of the café. "You know what happened to the buffalo man who tore out my eye? Now you wouldn't want the same thing to happen to you, would you, Donald?"

There couldn't be any better show, not even back in New York City with all them professional actor folk and such.

Donald was so worked up he looked ready to burst

while the sheriff was so calm and cool it looked like he could take a nap right on the spot.

But what could Donald do? The sheriff was in control of things as usual and the sheriff had just told him to go over and sit down and leave him alone till he was done eating.

And everybody knew how long it took for Sheriff Henry Burrell to eat.

Fargo quit running after a block. People noticed you when you ran in town. They knew something was wrong, and were liable to report you if they happened to bump into a lawman.

But even walking, people kept looking at him. He kept his head low but not even that helped much. His memory was still the problem. It was funny the way he could remember some things and not remember others. He had this picture of a horse, an Ovaro stallion, real clear in his mind. Was it his horse? And where was the horse now? And would it be somewhere he could see it?

He stopped two kids who were tossing a baseball back and forth. They threw it gently. Neither had ball gloves.

One kid, who was maybe seven, said, "Boy, mister, somebody really beat you up."

"Yeah, I guess they did. Either of you boys know where the livery is in town?"

The other kid said, "My older brother Steve, he got beat up real good just the way you did. He had to stay in bed for a week. The doc wouldn't even let him get up to pee."

"That's too bad," Fargo said. "Now how about the livery?"

The first boy pointed. "See that open door down there? That's the back of it."

"Thanks, son."

When you walked behind three blocks worth of

buildings you got a different impression of a town. You saw the latrines, the outhouses, the bonfires, the heaps of garbage and refuse. Not exactly what the mayor would want you to see.

A couple of sad, elderly horses ate some sad, elderly grass that the sun had turned brown. They stood indolent out behind the open door from which the clang of steel on steel—hammer on anvil—resounded on the clear morning air. Another stray memory: he'd seen the front of this place at some point before last night. The list of services the blacksmith offered were impressive: he'd shoe your horse, cut your hair, and forge and shape "pots-pans-plowshares." A Renaissance handyman.

The clanging, it turned out, came from the front of the large, barnlike interior. The blacksmith faced the front. And with all the noise and concentration he brought to his various tasks, he didn't seem to be aware of Fargo slipping in the back door and finding the big stallion he'd pictured.

In fact, the blacksmith didn't turn around until Fargo had found the right saddle and saddlebags and fixed them on the horse and mounted up.

At which point, an old man, with a face shaped by an enormous chaw of tobacco, came in the back door and said, "Mornin', stranger" just loud enough for the blacksmith to hear between clangs on the anvil.

"Hey!" the blacksmith hollered and flung down his hammer. A burly man with a huge mustache that marked him as a person of some vanity, the blacksmith grabbed his rifle and shouted, "You don't take that horse till you pay me!"

But it was hard to pay somebody when you didn't have any money. Fargo had been careful to check for any kind of ready currency in his pockets. He didn't have as much as a coin. And he didn't have the time nor inclination to argue with the blacksmith because that would lead to only one thing—the blacksmith would hold him at gunpoint and sic the law on him for being a deadbeat.

Fargo did the only thing he could.

He rode fast and hard out the back door.

The blacksmith rushed at him, firing nuisance shots. Fargo was already out of range.

He rode. No idea where he was going. No idea where he was, exactly. Memories of this town came to him in useless fragments. Not only didn't he know who he was, he didn't know why he was on this horse or how he'd gotten to this town in the first place.

The horse had been taken care of. That was the only thing he could be glad about. Fed and rested, the horse was in good shape for being ridden hard.

It was half an hour before Fargo stopped. He saw the glint of a small lake between a heavy cover of trees and undergrowth. It was almost as if it was a secret lake, the special province of a single individual.

Fargo ground-tied his horse and tiptoed his way over to a campfire where coffee boiled in a pot. His stomach twisted. Coffee would be so good.

He was distracted by the sound of splashing. He walked into the trees and undergrowth that had blocked his sight of the lake. What he saw was something out of a half-waking dream. One of the most silken-fleshed young women he'd ever seen was just now swimming to shore, her feet kicking hard to propel her body faster. He gulped. Would she be completely naked, as she appeared to be?

Be damned. She was even *more* naked than naked. She stood on the shallow sandy shore pulling her long, dark hair back, wringing the water from it. The way she raised her slender arms also raised the full breasts that were made even more engaging by their generous, coffee-colored nipples. Water beads sparkled on the dark splendor of her pubic hair. Her long, perfectly shaped legs gleamed damply.

Despite his situation—could a posse be far behind?—

he felt himself stir with a profound need for this young woman.

She saw him then. Or did she?

Just as he'd been startled by her nakedness, he was now startled by the curious flatness of her eyes. She saw—but somehow didn't see.

"Is somebody there?"

He didn't want to scare her. He said in his gentlest voice, "Yes, miss. I'm here."

"What's your name?"

He hesitated. "I'm not sure."

"You're not sure of your own name?" She didn't sound afraid, simply curious.

"Not right now I'm not, miss. It's hard to explain."

"You have a nice voice. A kind one." Then: "I need a few minutes to get dressed. I should be embarrassed that you're seeing me this way but there isn't much I can do about it. Feel free to help yourself to some coffee."

"Thank you. I could use some."

The coffee tasted as good as it smelled. It had been made by an expert hand. He rolled himself a smoke and leaned back against a boulder. The day was so damned beautiful. Clear blue sky. Snow-tipped mountains in the distance. Butterfly and buffalo and raccoon and roaming wild dogs. A day to go fishing. To relax. Not a day to be so baffled by simply existing. Not a day to be so stomach-clenching scared.

So much turmoil. It was as if he had been newly born into a dark and dangerous world without any forewarning or knowledge of how to cope. Flung into a jungle of bad deeds and murky motives. With no way to know how to make any sense of it.

He heard her coming through the trees. She was so slim, she barely made any noise. When she came into the clearing, he saw that she was even prettier close up, with a freckled, girlish face of green eyes and an

24

open smile. It was difficult to forget that body that lay beneath the thin, faded gingham of her dress. She wore Indian moccasins.

And then he looked at the eyes again and for the first time realized what was so remarkable about her. The way she moved, with such casual self-confidence, despite the fact that she was blind. Blind. No cane. No dog. Not even any tentative hand feeling her way. She moved with the confidence of a sighted person.

"In case you're wondering, I can see a little bit. About five percent of my natural sight, my doctor says."

"I was wondering how you moved around so well."

"I can see just enough to know if there's something in my path. I don't see very well out of the sides of my eyes, though." She spoke her words with a smile. "In case you ever want to sneak up on me, the side is the best way."

"I'll remember that."

She helped herself to some coffee. She had a blanket spread out near the boulder where Fargo stood.

"Would you give me your hand?" she said.

"Beg pardon?"

"Your hand. Would you let me hold your hand for a minute?"

He laughed. "I'd have to charge you something for that privilege."

"I'm not trying to seduce you. I have second sight."

"I guess I don't know what that is."

"I don't, either. Not exactly, anyway. My mother had it, too, and I guess she sort of passed it on before she left us. She'd just touch somebody and she could tell a whole lot about 'em."

"Read their minds, you mean?"

"Not exactly. More like—like tell what their mood was and if they were being honest with her. She was blind, too. She couldn't see well enough to get a fix

25

on a person. She had to touch them in some way and then she could tell. Sort of like astrologers pretend to do. But I don't put much store by astrology. Do you?"

"I read my horoscope every day."

"You do?"

"I sure do. Right before I shine up my crystal ball."

Her laugh was soft. "You're a decent man. I can tell that already. Your humor is kind. A lot of people—well, their humor is mean." She extended her hand and he took it. "Now, if you don't mind, I'll get to know you a little better. And maybe I can tell you a few things about yourself that you don't know."

He said, "You can tell me my name for starters. That'd help me a lot."

All the money Stan Thayer made at his mortuary, you'd think he could pick up dead folks in something a little fancier than a buckboard that smelled of the cows he'd butchered out at his farm. But Stan—to the point of being a bitter joke to the townspeople—was what you'd call frugal. By which you meant cheap, by which you meant that the bastard wouldn't give a dying man a sip of water.

The other thing about Stan Thayer was that he liked to act official, especially if there was a murder involved. Way he strutted around in that tall, gangly, black-suited Ichabod Crane body of his, bony skeleton hands on the lapels of his suit coat, you'd think he was more important than Sheriff Burrell.

For instance, now.

Thayer led the two men who carried the sheet-covered body down the stairs. Then he stood next to the back of his buckboard. Every time one of the crowd would step forward to get a closer look, Stan would say, "You don't have no permission to get this close to an official vehicle. Now you get back in line." And he'd shoo them away with an imperious wave of his hand, as if he was running off a dog or a naughty child.

Sheriff Burrell shook his head when he saw Stan playing lord and master again. There were only two civic clubs in town and Stan had made sure that he was president of both. He was intolerable enough before getting himself elected—he basically bribed every single man with good liquor and good cigars to vote for him—but after he got elected, Burrell liked to joke that everybody should pitch in and buy Stan a crown so that way they'd know he was king.

Burrell said, "Stan, these people are citizens. They have a right to see what goes on in their town. Now you quit shooin' them away or I'll shoo *you* away."

Several in the crowd giggled. Even more glanced at their neighbor and nodded knowingly. Somebody had finally upbraided that damned Stan Thayer. They'd be telling this story at every saloon in town, and at every supper table, too.

Sheriff Burrell said to the crowd, "You know I like to keep people informed. So what I can tell you so far is that we found a young woman dead upstairs in the hotel. She'd been slid under the bed so nobody could see her or find her. We're not sure yet who she is. But that's the first thing we'll be doin'—finding out who she is and what she was doin' in town and how she came to stay in one of the biggest and fanciest suites in the hotel. And you can bet that soon as I find out anythin', you good folks'll be the first to know."

All Thayer could do—knowing he'd been publicly humiliated by Burrell—was glower at the lawman and plot how to bring him down. Thayer had seen a print in the blood on the hotel room floor that would expose Burrell for what he was. . . .

Maya, her name was. Maya Boatman. If that wasn't some kind of name, she laughed. She had been slowly losing her sight since age ten and was now twenty.

She would probably end up an old maid even though she was quite pretty, she knew as much be-

27

cause people always told her so. Still, no man had come forward to ask for her hand. She would be a burden. A woman was expected to work with the strength and acumen of an ox. There was only so much a blind woman could do in ways that being pretty didn't matter. . . .

Her favorite thing was to pack a small picnic and spend the day outdoors, away from her drunken and mean brother. Sometimes, physically mean.

But that was enough about her, she said. Now they would talk about him.

She fed him, coffeed him, and then sat beneath a huge oak and tended to his wounds. She bathed the wounds, bled them a little, and then daubed them with a piece of clean cloth she'd brought along from home. She said she'd heard of people forgetting who they were but couldn't think of the word for it. She thought it happened when an especially hard blow had been struck on the person's head. She thought he would probably be all right if he hadn't already gone into convulsions or started passing out all the time. Of course, she couldn't be sure of any of this, because she wasn't a doctor, nor even a nurse. All her "wisdom" was just things she'd overheard from time to time.

She went through as many Christian names as she could think of, from Aaron to Zeb. None of them sounded right.

While she was doing this, he did something he would have thought impossible. She had eased his fear and disorientation so much that he drifted into the deep sleep he'd been deprived of last night. When he woke, his just-opened eyes saw a quarter-moon imprinted on the dusk sky. The night creatures were just now announcing themselves with the sounds that would be baleful when full dark came.

But that wasn't all. She had managed to slide him over on to the blanket she'd brought along and now she lay next to him, stroking his groin to bring every part of his body fully alert. "I had a lover once. He moved away. I never thought I'd be interested in another man until I heard you speak today."

The musk of her womanliness filled his senses. He responded with an erection so stiff it threatened to rip through his buckskins. He wouldn't have thought he could become so aroused in his condition but the woman's breasts pressing against his chest—the feel of her stiff nipples, the luxurious fullness of her breasts themselves—made him groan deeply with pleasure and desire.

Fargo was a man who made a point of pleasing his women. He considered having sex not only a pleasure but a privilege. The taste, the scent, the warm flesh of women were things to be treated like a great gift from the gods.

Maya, for instance, was a treasure trove of curves and coves and hidden places. He reached down and pressed his hand against the moist fullness of her womanhood. Even through the fabric of her dress, he could feel the hot tender lips of her pleasure. The tip of his finger sought the point at the top of her legs where a woman would be all yours if you were skillful and patient and tender enough. She responded with a full body surge of enjoyment, a kind of crazed writhing that gave promise to how she'd respond when she was naked.

She was in the best sense a tease—a knowing tease—using her mouth and fingers to bring him to a bucking ecstasy even before she managed to free his growing manliness and set her mouth to making it even harder and fuller.

Then her hands were moving nimbly to slide up her dress so that she could straddle his face and let him return the pleasure she had so freely given.

The shy, peaceful woman remained quiet enough but she was shy no longer. She let his tongue drive her into a kind of insanity as she began to ride him the way she would an animal. His tongue never ceased making her hotter and hotter as he tasted the golden nectar that was starting to run down his chin. Fargo's hands were engaged now, holding her hips and helping her to find the exact balance she needed. When she could handle no more she made a sound that was part moan and part muffled scream. Fargo didn't relent. His tongue kept giving her joy until she fell away from him, fell on her back with her legs parted and her sex open to him.

Now it was his turn for pleasure and he certainly took it, driving deeper and deeper and faster and faster until he had to wonder where all this strength was coming from. But he didn't wonder long, his strong hands cupping her buttocks and grinding her into him so that he could go even deeper. Her mouth was a furnace of desire, her skillful tongue keeping a rhythm with her hips and buttocks as Fargo rammed and jammed his way home.

Then they lay next to each other, spent with pure, heady joy, sated in the innocent way that animals are sated after the sex act. With simple, uncomplicated carnal abandon.

4

The town had many distinctions, not the least of which was its gallows. Made of fine oak, it was stout, sturdy, and as fine as anything in this vale of tears. It stood right next to the two-story stone court house, a statement to all of mankind that this was a town not afraid of quick and absolute justice. There was even talk of adding a second rope so that when—as was the case with the Harper brothers—there were two miscreants, they could be executed at the exact same time.

Now a sign stood in front of the gallows:

HANGING
5:30 P.M.
DANCE TO FOLLOW

A local sketch artist stood in front of the gallows now, penciling out a rather inept depiction of the hanging mechanism. He was a butcher by day but drew for pleasure—his own.

A hanging. Everybody was going to have a danged good time.

Maya fixed Fargo a place in the barn loft. "I'm not sure what my brother'll do if he finds you here. So be real quiet."

She'd brought him a couple of blankets and laid

them out on the hay. And also some slices of dried beef, bread, and some beer.

"You need more rest."

"I need to find out what happened last night. And who I am."

"Rest, first. You're still pretty wobbly when you walk. And then tomorrow I'll find out who you are."

He smiled. "I know you can handle yourself and all but just how do you plan to do that?"

"I'll go into town the way I usually do and all I'll hear about is that dead girl they found under the bed in the hotel. And then I'll hear all about the man the law is looking for. And that'll be you. I'll pick up as much information as I can. And by tomorrow afternoon, you'll be fit enough to start figuring things out."

"You could get in trouble."

"For what? Asking questions? People think I'm helpless. And so they trust me. I think they think I'm pretty dumb. They wouldn't think I could be helping out the man everybody's looking for."

"You're taking a chance."

"Believe it or not, I'm having fun."

"You are?"

"Sure—back there by the lake—what we did. That was fun. And this is fun. It's like solving a mystery in a book. There's this woman in town, she used to read to me, especially mysteries. And that's what this is."

"There's one difference."

"What's that?"

"That stories in books can't hurt you. But this is life and that's very different." He paused. He had to say it, had to hear himself admit the possibility. Because it *was* a possibility. "What if it turns out that I'm the killer?"

"You're not the killer."

"How do you know that?"

"I can tell about people."

"You're never wrong?"

"Well, sometimes, I guess."

"What if you're wrong about me? What if it turns out you've been helping a killer all along? If I'm the man who killed that woman I saw under the bed—I don't think I'd want to live, anyway, something like that on my mind."

Neither spoke for a time. He looked at the night in the open window slots. The brilliant indifferent stars and the lazy quarter-moon made for a melancholy moment. The smell of hay still wet in places from the last rain—the sweet-sour tang of horse manure—the soft sawn smell of the new lumber on the sliding barn door downstairs. He allowed himself the luxury of having a moment's peace. He didn't give a damn about any of it for that moment. There was just this very pretty blind girl and the summoning of his soft hay mattress and her hint that everything would be all right. . . .

Without quite knowing what he was doing, he lay back, as if pressed in that direction by a giant, gentle, invisible hand . . . and gave into his sudden exhaustion . . . and the sudden stabbing headache that told him he was still suffering from what Maya had called a concussion. . . .

And then he slept . . .

"You recognize this, mister?"

At first he couldn't make out much of the man standing over him with the rifle pointed at his face.

"Yep. I sure do."

"My sister bring you here?"

"No. I just saw your barn and—"

The man didn't use his rifle. He used his foot. He brought it up fast. It didn't connect square on the jaw as he'd apparently planned but it caught plenty hard on the side. Enough to send shock after echoing shock of pain up the side of Fargo's face.

"Now you tell me the truth, you sumbitch."

"Tal! Tal! No!"

Maya's voice coming from the far side of the barn. In his mind Fargo pictured her making her way through the darkness. That sure wouldn't help her blindness any.

Tal made the mistake of turning. Maybe it wouldn't have been a mistake with somebody slower and less angry and frustrated than Fargo. But it sure was a mistake with him.

Tal was in just the right position so that Fargo's kick would catch him where any man is most vulnerable. He screamed when Fargo's boot tip connected with its target. His rifle fired. He would have blown Fargo's head apart if Fargo hadn't already flung himself to his feet—forgetting his pain—and smashed four quick fists into Tal's face.

Tal swung a looping right hand that not only missed Fargo but left him off balance. His arms started waving helplessly as he lost his footing on the edge of the loft. Then his rifle went flying through the air, landing on the dirt floor below, and firing uselessly into the gloom.

Tal followed his rifle. No amount of screaming, cursing, wailing, or flailing could save him from falling off the loft edge—especially when Fargo, out to defend himself at all cost—gave him a slight shove.

Fortunately, the fall wasn't enough to do any permanent damage, though it probably didn't do much for Tal's own inner savage. Any man who beat up his sister—especially his *blind* sister—probably thought of himself as a pretty tough hombre. Falling off a barn loft hopefully would knock him down a peg or two.

Fargo took the old-fashioned route. He climbed down the ladder. Maya was ministering to her brother. "Oh, Tal, you always have to get so mad."

"He's the one they're lookin' for, Sis."

"That who's looking for?"

"The whole town. Including the sheriff."

"What's he supposed to've done?"

"There's no s'posed to—"

And then Tal, who hadn't yet regained his feet, told of how this here man, name of Skye Fargo, had been seen with blood all over him running from the fancy hotel room where the dead girl was. And how everybody was looking for him and that word was he was in town to help one of his buddies, a fella named Cates. He also described how the girl had been so badly beaten and mutilated.

"Then it couldn't have been him, Tal."

"Oh, no? Why not?"

"He wouldn't do by a woman like that."

Tal laughed. "Oh, yeah, he looks like a real gentle type, he does."

"He sure is with women, Tal. That I can testify to."

Tal started to struggle to his feet. Fargo put out a hand, helped him up.

Tal said, "I coulda broken my back."

"That's true. But you could've busted my head wide open. I didn't have any choice."

Tal sulked a moment and said, "Well, he ain't stayin' here. If Sheriff Burrell ever found out we were puttin' him up—"

"One more day," Maya said, "just till he starts getting his strength back."

Fargo said, "I appreciate that, Maya. But I've got things I've got to do." He turned to Tal. "You say I came here to help a friend of mine by the name of Cates?"

"That's how I heard it, mister. Curt Cates. Only he's already behind bars."

"Where do I find his house?"

Tal told him where Serena Cates lived. "But you'd be crazy to leave here now. They'd spot you in a minute."

"Not in the middle of the night, they wouldn't."

"You can't go now, Skye," Maya said. "You're not strong enough."

"I'm feeling a lot better after all the sleeping I did today and tonight." He still felt dizzy but he'd be damned if he'd admit it to her. "I'd like to get going, in fact."

"Oh, Skye—"

"Dammit, if he wants to go, Maya—"

"You just want to get rid of him, Tal!"

"I just don't want to get crosswise with Burrell. I sure don't want him as an enemy."

Fargo went over to Maya and took her gently by the shoulders. "I'll be fine. And Tal's just being practical. There's no reason for either of you to get into trouble over this. Why get dragged into it?"

"But if they see you they'll shoot on sight."

"There's a reward," Tal said. "Three thousand dollars. That's more than most folks make in three years. She's right about that, mister. They'll shoot you on sight. That's somethin' you need to be careful of."

Tal sounded as if he was giving his advice sincerely. You never could figure people. Here was a guy who beat up his blind sister. Here was a guy Fargo had pushed off a barn loft. And here was a guy telling him to avoid getting killed.

As if he'd been able to read Fargo's mind, he said, "I don't want nothin' to happen to you 'cause if it does, that's all Sis'll talk about the rest of our lives. And she'll blame me."

"You're darn right, I will, Tal."

Tal went back up to the house. Fargo went down to the creek and washed in the cold, clean water. His big stallion needed to be saddled and fed. Maya insisted on taking care of those things for him while he ate bread and drank the coffee she'd fixed for him.

"I need to find out who the dead girl was," Fargo said.

"Tal said she was a prostitute."

"She was a rich one, staying in a fancy hotel like that."

"I doubt she signed for the room."

"Yeah, I doubt that, too. Somebody else did. That's something else I need to find out."

"How'll you get around without people recognizing you?"

"I won't be able to. Not for long. But Serena Cates can find things out for me.

"I'm scared for you, Skye."

"I appreciate that. But I'm a lot more scared for Curt."

Sheriff Henry Burrell got up and went out onto the front stoop of his three-room house and sat there smoking his pipe and looking up at the stars.

He was trying not to go into the woods.

He was trying not to think about the dead girl in the hotel room.

He was trying not to think about how he got sometimes when he drank too much.

The sounds of a lonely dog, an alert barn owl, and a night bird's mating call kept him company.

The temperature had dropped well into the lower sixties. He sat shirtless in wrinkled work trousers and bare feet. The quarter-moon was so sharply etched it looked unreal, almost like a painting on a stage backdrop. He enjoyed this time of night, having *learned* to enjoy it after the death of his wife had left him empty and vaguely frightened in the middle of the night. For some reason, sitting on the stoop and taking in the scents and sights and sounds of a cool summer midnight brought him solace. As if the shadows eased not only his grief but his remorse.

If he could only go back and change things . . . Steffanie just fell face forward dead one evening at the supper table. All he could think of was all the times he had run around on her . . . nobody was in a better position to have free whores pushed at him than the town sheriff. The gals who ran those houses—and there were three of them in town here—wanted to keep the lawmen happy. And so they lent them their best gals for as long of an evening as they wanted them. But they'd soon learned about Henry and how he got when he was drunk. . . .

It wasn't so bad when he bruised them if the bruises didn't show. Sometimes he could control himself to the degree that he'd visit his fists and teeth only on their bodies. It was when he got rough with their faces that the madams got pissed. That, as one of them had angrily explained, was like walking into a general store and damaging the merchandise to the point that nobody wanted to buy it.

There weren't a lot of men who wanted a whore with a black eye.

Steffanie had to suffer through all of it. And then their son Hap turning out the way he had—the sullen town bully who drank just as much and pounded women around just as much as the old man—she'd already seen Hap starting to do these things when he was a strapping youngster.

The night bird again. An almost chilling cry this time. Coming from the woods.

He decided he'd better go have a look.

Make sure they were still where he'd dug the hole and put them. Sometimes a raccoon could dig up the deepest hole a man could put in the ground.

He stood up. Thought a moment about going in to get his boots. Decided he was being a nancy boy about it and moved on. Hell, a few broken twigs against the bottoms of his feet—was he such a pampered sissy at this age that he couldn't take a few gnarled twigs jagging him in the soles of his feet?

Hell no, he wasn't.

He went to see if the bloody clothes from last night were still where he'd buried them.

A few lanterns gleamed in the windows of the town's poorer houses on the edge of town. These people lived a life that combined town and country. They were well enough away from neighbors that they could keep a dairy cow or two plus chickens and a few pigs in their back yards without making anybody mad. They kept farmers' hours, too, which meant that they had just risen now that first light appeared in pale streaks across the night sky.

Fargo ground-tied his stallion a quarter-mile from the Cates place. The law would naturally assume that he would try and contact Serena Cates for help. He'd apparently come here to help her and her husband.

That meant that the law would also have posted a man somewhere near the house, a man waiting patiently for Fargo to show up.

Fargo did a wide sweep of all sides of the log cabin where the Cates family lived. He didn't find anything suspicious as he walked the south, east, and west points of the property. Then he heard the *plop plop plop* of acorns falling from a tree. A man was up there, moving around. He no doubt had a rifle and he no doubt intended to kill Fargo. But Fargo was too far away to fire on. The shooter had to hope that Fargo would do him the favor of moving closer.

Fargo turned and walked to the west, as if he was heading into town. The mud road was rutted from recent rains. The cool air smelled of flapjacks being made on a nearby stove. Horses, dogs, and kids would be coming awake soon.

A large oak ten feet off the road gave Fargo the hiding place he was looking for. He hurried behind it. Drew his Colt and waited.

The shooter was a tall man with a limp. He didn't

wear a hat so Fargo got a look at his face. The man looked sad. You didn't expect a shooter to look sad. By rights, a shooter should look serene stalking his prey. The way hunters looked at peace. Probably the limp, Fargo decided. Anything that marks a man as different also marks him as an inferior. And inferiors are never quite accepted by people. They might feel sorry for the inferiors, they might even encourage and help the inferiors, but the inferiors always know that they aren't looked on as being as whole and desirable as their smiling and patronizing benefactors. Hence, the man's sad face.

Fargo was about to make that face even sadder.

He let the limping man get several feet past the oak tree before making his move. Then he ran fast at the man. The shooter heard him, turned to fire, but it was already too late. Fargo grabbed the barrel of the man's rifle and ripped it from his hands.

Fargo tucked it under his arm. With his Colt, he beckoned for the shooter to start walking back toward the Cates cabin. The sad-faced man looked as if he wanted to say something. But he didn't. The defeat that was on his face now spread throughout his body. The shoulders slumped, the arms dangled limp, and the head hung low. He wasn't going to be any more trouble.

Fargo and the man went to the cabin door. Serena answered in a plain, loose dress that somehow lent her pretty, earnest face a kind of prairie nobility. Fargo asked for some rope. She stared a moment at the man next to Fargo and said, "That's Bryce Willis."

"He with the sheriff?"

"Sometimes. When the sheriff needs an extra hand. He goes to the same church I do. He's a decent man, Skye."

Fargo snorted. Learning his own name was a step in the right direction. "Unless he's shooting people in the back."

"I wouldn't never backshoot nobody," Willis said. "Not even a killer like you."

Fargo smiled. "I have my doubts about that, Willis. About you not backshooting anybody. But I'm not going to give you the chance to prove it either way. Now, c'mon, I'll tie you up."

"He hasn't had an easy life, Skye." Her dark, compassionate eyes rested momentarily on Willis's bad foot. "You know what I mean."

"I'm sorry for his bad life, Serena. But that doesn't mean he wouldn't have shot me in the back."

"I don't see how you can do much asking around now, Skye," Serena Cates said, bringing him a cup of coffee.

"I don't have any choice," Fargo said.

"But how'll you get around with everybody looking for you, Skye?"

"Won't be easy but I'll have to do it."

"Didn't anything come of the dead girl's sister Barb Potter? I know she took over her father's farm. You mentioned when you first got to town that you were going to see her but never got around to it."

He hadn't told her yet. He said, "I need you to tell me who I am."

She started to smile then stopped herself. "Skye, what're you talking about?"

He touched his head. "Somebody hit me pretty hard and my memory—certain things are still clear to me. But I don't have any recollection of who *I* am."

"Oh, my Lord, Skye. My Lord."

She reached across the crude kitchen table—the wobbly kitchen table—and said, "I'll help you all I can."

It was just then that Tommy socked Davie and the cabin was filled with sudden tears and screams.

Being a lawman had taught him that getting rid of bloody clothing was never as easy as it seemed. Burrell had seen any number of killers caught by shirts and trousers that suddenly turned up. You could throw them in the river but a lot of times they'd surface again. You could burn them but sometimes enough of a shirt, say, would be left to tell you who the killer was. Or you could bury them. Burying seemed the most reliable to Burrell.

The bloody shirt and trousers he'd buried had been seen around town so often that nobody who lived hereabouts would have any trouble knowing who they belonged to.

He'd buried them off-trail, nearly three feet down, and covered the loose dirt with branches and leaves.

What he hadn't counted on was how unsettling this was, having the garments so near the house. It was as if the clothes radiated an invisible signal that made it difficult to sleep or to think about anything else.

There they were, buried underground. And there he was eating supper or relaxing with his pipe or darning his socks for the next day—and the strange unseen, unheard *vibration* that the bloody clothes gave off clogged his mind.

He needed to know they were safe. Then maybe he could get an hour or two of sleep before the day began. He couldn't go on this way much longer, he was sure of that.

Maybe if he moved the clothes—bury them further away from the house—

The earth of loam, the earth of sandy soil, the earth of tiny bones of animals from eons ago—so many secrets in its cold embrace.

The bloody clothes buried by Henry Burrell were just one more.

He stumbled through the undergrowth beneath the paling sky. And when he saw them, a gasp almost like a sob filled his throat.

Nothing—not forest creature nor man—had

touched them. The branches and leaves that covered their grave were perfectly in place.

Safe—his dread and fear had been for nothing.

"I'll be all right for a while and then it'll hit me," Fargo was saying. "That I don't know who I am. That I have memories of some things but none of others." He pressed his fingers against his temples. "And the damned headache. Sometimes that's the worst part of all."

"You need to see a doctor."

"I see a doctor, he goes straight to the sheriff as soon as I leave."

"You're really sweating."

"This fever. It comes and goes."

"Why don't you rest here for a while?"

He smiled grimly. "You're forgetting I've got a duly sworn deputy sheriff tied up and gagged in your back-yard. They'll come looking for him pretty soon. I'd hate to be sawing logs when they come. I'm sorry I dragged you into this."

Now it was her turn for a grim smile. "Dragged me into it? Skye, they're about to hang my husband. I'm already in it."

"I'm sure I asked you this before," Fargo said. "But if I did, I don't remember. Does Curt have any enemies?"

"Oh, gosh, Skye. Curt? No."

"Think about it, Serena. I don't necessarily mean anybody who picked a fight with him or anything like that. But somebody who might have a reason to resent him."

This time, she didn't answer right away. "Well, Paul, I guess."

"Paul?"

"Paul O'Brien."

"He and Curt have some kind of run-in?"

"Not a run-in exactly. But—well, it was about me.

43

I—well, I went out with Paul a few times. Paul is a very nice man. But he's got this terrible temper. He thought I'd marry him."

"Terrible temper enough to kill a girl and make it look like Curt did it?"

"I can't say yes and I can't say no. I told Sheriff Burrell about him, of course. But I don't think he even approached Paul about anything."

"Where's this O'Brien live?"

She told him.

"If he was the killer, then he wouldn't have been happy about me showing up and looking into things."

"No, he wouldn't have."

"Maybe I forced his hand."

"How so?"

"Maybe I forced him to kill that girl in the hotel room and then set me up for it."

"But that's so cold-blooded—" She shook her head. Then stopped. Fargo could see that she'd remembered something. "He loosened a wheel on our wagon one night."

"When was this?"

"A year ago or so. One of the boys recognized him running away from the shed where we store things. We couldn't figure out what he would've been doing. We didn't check the wagon. We went to a dance that night—practically everyone in town had gone—and halfway there, the wheel came loose. It was one of the few times I'd ever seen Curt so mad he actually confronted somebody. Paul denied having anything to do with the wheel. Curt called him a liar. Paul started to swing at Curt but a couple of the older men stepped in and stopped the fight before it really got started."

"Was that the last run-in you had with O'Brien?"

"Well, our shed mysteriously caught fire one night."

"Any proof it was O'Brien?"

"No proof. But a strong suspicion."

Fargo finished up his coffee. "He ever make any advances to you?"

"A few times. I never told Curt about them. I didn't want him to have any more run-ins. Paul's a lot bigger than Curt and a lot angrier. Sometimes, he acts almost crazy, in fact, when he doesn't get his own way, times like that."

"Then I'm definitely going to pay him a little courtesy visit."

"You'll have your hands full."

He looked down at the directions he'd scrawled out on a piece of paper with a lead pencil. Despite his memory loss and his slamming headache, he had a lot of work ahead of him. He said, "I just realized something."

"What's that?"

"I'm gonna be damned interested in hearing *why* I supposedly killed that woman in the hotel room." A flash of anger. "My sense of things is that I never saw her before I woke up on the floor in the room. But my memory—I can't know that for sure."

She touched her work-worn hand to his. "Oh, Skye, I wish there was something I could do—some way I could help you."

"You've helped me plenty already. These two names sound like good leads." He stood up. He still wasn't the old Skye Fargo. The old Skye Fargo's knees didn't tremble when he stood up. He hit his head with the tips of his fingers. Angry. Like hitting a machine that wouldn't work right. Very angry, in fact.

5

People would say he was downright strange if they ever found out what he did.

But then people found undertaker Stan Thayer strange, anyway.

He slept in a house that usually had a corpse or two on the premises, for one thing. And for another thing—and maybe most suspicious of all—he talked to his corpses and he didn't care who knew it.

Talked—to his corpses.

A fella could walk in any time during the day and trundle on back to the room where Thayer gussied up the dead folk. And then stand there and listen to him jabber.

Well, you sure picked a nice day to pass, Mrs. Williamson. Rain and cold and fog. That's the kind of day I hope to pass, myself.

Sure hope you divided your farm equal among those two hotheaded boys of yours, Mr. Englinger. Otherwise those two'll tear each other apart.

You're the prettiest gal I ever buried, Ruth. You're pretty even lyin' here right now. I always wanted to ask you out but I just never could work up the nerve. Now I sure wish I'd've done it. Yes, ma'am, I sure do.

The dead woman Stanley Jerome Thayer was talking to now was the one they'd hauled out of the hotel room. From under the bed. Some man named Fargo was being sought for her murder.

But you and I know a little secret, don't we, lady? That Fargo, he didn't kill you, did he? No, sir, he didn't. Because if you happen to know what you're looking at, the way I do, you notice things like those bloody footprints over in the corner where you were killed—before you were dragged under the bed. I saw this Fargo's footprints. They were real plain to see. He didn't kill you. His footprints weren't over there in the corner where you were butchered. But the killer's were. And we know who those footprints belong to, don't we, lady? Yes, ma'am, they tracked your blood from the corner to the bed. Plain as day. And you know what? The killer knew about those tracks, too; or at least figured it out later. Because the killer came back, my yes, came back bold as brass. But the blood on the floor was still drying so I saw the fresh tracks and compared them to the old tracks. So now Stan Thayer knows who the killer is. I'm not a braggin' man, but I knew if I waited long enough—Well, lady, there are people in this town who disrespect me, who make fun of me every chance they get. One person in particular. And, well, we'll see what happens when—

"If you talked to live people as much as you do dead people, you'd have a whole lot more friends, Stan," Abner Thompson said from the doorway.

Thayer said, "You snuck up on me again, Ab."

"So who really killed her?"

"Huh?"

"What you said to the dead lady there."

"Oh."

"And she had some body, didn't she?"

"Yeah," Thayer said, looking down at the corpse. "Yeah, she sure did."

"So who killed her?" Ab, who was at least seventy, leaned in the doorway with his corncob pipe, his lurid red suspenders, his filthy clothes handmade from thrown-away feed sacks, and said, "And don't say you didn't say it 'cause I heard ya."

"Don't count what you say to dead people," Thayer said.

"Oh? How come?"

"How come? 'Cause they're *dead* is how come. They can't hear anything you say."

"Then if they can't hear ya, why do ya talk to 'em in the first place?"

Good old Abe. He could drive a mind crazy, he could.

"You just forget what I said, Ab."

Ab giggled. "My age, I forget just about everything."

"Good."

Ab pushed away from the door frame, stood up straight. "Just wonderin' if you could use some help today." Ab never worked for whiskey alone. Several belts of whiskey was more like it.

"Guess you could sweep off the porch and do some dustin' in the parlor there."

"Mind if I help myself to a drink first?"

Thayer looked up from the dead woman's hair, which he'd been pulling a comb through. "One drink. Then afterward you can have more. But no more than one now. You get drunk, your work isn't worth a damn, Ab, and you know it."

"I'll just have one, Thayer." He grinned his ghoulish old man grin. "A real big one."

"And you forget anything you heard me say to this here dead woman, Ab," he said to Ab's back as the old man set off to take the bottle down from the kitchen cupboard.

Sheriff Henry Burrell was finishing up his first cup of coffee for the day when he heard the footsteps on the back stoop and the door jerk open. Various kinds of weather had warped the door frame over the years so that when you opened it now, you had to use enough force to give the entire small house a jolt that vibrated through the walls.

Burrell's back was to his son Hap as Hap came through the door. The combined stench of cheap liquor and cheap perfume preceded him into the kitchen. He stood in the doorway, grinning and giving a cocky little salute off his Stetson. Then he sniffed the air. He was always hungry when he came home this way. Nothing a drunk likes better at a time like this than a stomach-filling meal right before he drops down an eight-hour chasm of sleep.

Hap had been coming home this way for the past four years. Always smirky, always with a sense of superiority about him, as if his old man was just one more stranger to be treated with his usual contempt. He'd had innumerable jobs over that period. But inevitably, after a month or two, the new employer would stop by the sheriff's office looking guilty and say that he was sorry but that, uh—shit, Henry, I hate to say it—but that boy of yours just ain't gonna work out. The employers would never say why exactly, but later Burrell would hear stories about playing dice or fighting or sneaking corn liquor into the workplace. A couple of employers even got treated to Hap's hard fists when he was hung over and in no mood to take orders from anybody.

Hap even tried a couple of distant towns—at his old man's insistence. There was a time that Burrell got so embarrassed by all the jobs that Hap had lost, he shipped him off to Boulder Pass and Junction City, setting him up in advance with employers there. But it was always the same. Hap'd get drunk and get fired. And Hap didn't like the notion that he was nobody. Here, he was the sheriff's son and he never let anybody forget it. The old man would defend him no matter what. But in a strange town—who knew or who cared about Hap Burrell? So he'd always come back hangdog and full of promises to behave himself, to get a job and keep it this time, and to help the old man when the old man needed it. Keeping the yard up would be a good start, Burrell said. So Hap, he kept it up a time or two but after that, back to his drinking and fighting and girl-impregnating, he was the old happy Hap and Burrell was just old and sad.

Even hung over, even tired out as he had to be, Hap was still the slick, boyish, handsome lad he always was. Did he ever run out of that so-called charm of his?

Hap never waited for the old man to start in on him. He'd learned young that the best way to deal with Henry was to start right in on him with the charm.

"Saw Tim Perry last night, makin' his rounds," Hap said.

"Tim's the best lawman I got."

Hap snorted. "You wish he was your son, don't you?"

Burrell looked at him. "He wouldn't give me the heartache you do, if that's what you mean. I made him a deputy a year ago and he's run things just fine. Never had a deputy I could trust like him."

Hap said, "Maybe you could adopt him."

Hap had an unceasing jealousy where Deputy Tim Perry was concerned. Burrell used to try and hide his pride in Tim from Hap. But no more.

Hap decided to try buttering up the old man, change the mood.

"You should've been over at the Brass Rail last night, Pa," Hap said. You could still see where rouge and powder streaked his cheeks. "Some of the boys there started talking about lawmen. And they ended up saying you were the best in the whole territory."

"They did, huh?"

"They sure did."

"A lot of them still wearing dresses?"

"Huh?"

"The boys at the Brass Rail. All the rouge you got streaked all over you, I figured the boys there must've been got up as girls."

"Oh." Hap drew a finger down his cheek, examined it. Rubbed a thumb against it. "Oh. I forgot. I stopped by to see Betty Ward."

"Think you'll get her pregnant again, do you?"

"How'd you know—"

Sheriff Henry Burrell then did what Hap always dreaded he would do. Lost his temper. It was a thunderous Old Testament temper. The sort of temper that would send even grizzlies running for cover.

Henry announced his loss of patience—his frustration with his irresponsible son—by bringing down a fist as big as a small pumpkin and smashing it against the wood table. Cracks raced down the surface—fissures of separated wood—joining those that had been put there during previous outbursts.

"How do I know? How the hell do you think I know? Because the time she came over here at three o'clock in the morning and woke you up, she woke me up, too. You think I couldn't hear her crying? You think I couldn't hear her threaten to tell her folks? You think I couldn't hear her screaming that you had to marry her?"

"But Pa, it worked out all right. It—"

"Shut up!"

"Yes, Pa," he mumbled in that chastised little-boy tone that was almost as aggravating as his contrived charm at its worst.

"I know the rest of it, too. Because she woke me up a week later when she came over to tell you that her 'monthly visitor' had finally come and she wasn't pregnant, after all."

"I told her she wasn't. We were careful and—"

"Yeah, real careful, I bet." He glowered. "In five

51

years, I plan to retire. If things go right, they'll give me a little pension and I can spend my last years fishing and enjoying myself. There'll be a new man here and all the headaches'll be his. There's only one thing that could put a crimp in my plan."

"Pa, listen—"

"And that's you. *You* could put a crimp in it. You could do somethin' so stupid and so embarrassing that they'd run us both out of town. They've cut me a lot of slack where you're concerned. They've all got kids and they know how kids can be. They know that no matter how good a parent is, a wild one can come along—most of the time it's a boy, but every once in a while, it's a girl—a wild one can come along and the parents can't do anything about it. The wild one does exactly what he wants to and everybody around him tries to be understanding with the parents—they know that the wild one could just as easily have been theirs—but one day this one wild child does something so bad that the town can't forgive it. And on that day, everybody turns on both him and his parents."

"Pa, please—"

"And that's going to happen with us. I can feel it. I have nightmares about it. Three, four times a day I get sick to my stomach—all twisted up and my throat burning with bile—thinking about you and all the trouble you've gotten into over the years."

"You're not being fair to me, Pa." Cunning came into his eyes. His voice didn't change. His posture didn't change. He sat in the chair across from his old man without moving at all. But still there was this—change. He wiped his paw across his nice, store-bought shirt—he rolled around with some girl last night and the shirt was a wrinkled, stained mess anyway—and then said, "I'm not the only one better be careful, Pa."

Now that his temper had quelled some, Burrell could hear nuances again, subtle hints you could pick up only if you listened carefully. That was the change. For the first part of the conversation—where Burrell had been tearing into Hap—Hap had assumed the posture of the browbeaten boy. He had taken his father's insults without any real argument.

"What's that supposed to mean, Hap? That you're not the only one better be careful? You talking about me?"

Before Hap could explain himself, a knock came on the front door. Hap practically leapt up from his chair, eager to get away from the table.

He stalked through the small house and jerked open the front door.

Marva Delaney, the middle-aged woman who lived down the street, said, "Well, that mangy mutt's been at it again." She sounded ready to cry.

"Oh, Mrs. Delaney, not your roses." He sounded as sappy-sad as a bad actor. Part of his "charm."

"My *prize* roses."

"You hear that, Pa?" Hap shouted too loudly, as if his old man was in Europe or something. "Mrs. Delaney's prize roses."

"I heard." Burrell sighed. This wasn't a good time for Marva Delaney to appear. Actually, when he thought about it, there was *no* good time for Marva Delaney to appear. But despite all the wild and woolly tales of a lawman's life, most of it was not spent in gunfights and feats of derring-do . . . most of it was spent in dealing with the Marva Delaneys of the world.

Burrell pushed away from the table, rose, worked out a couple of kinks in his back and then walked over to the door.

"It's King again, Sheriff," the woman said. She would have been attractive except for the huge mole on her chin. She had more hair growing out of it than could be found on Burrell's head.

"You sure it was King, Mrs. Delaney?" This particular morning, Burrell didn't even *try* to hide his grumpiness.

"Of *course* it was King, Sheriff. Who *else* would it be if it wasn't King? King's always around our yard, just waiting for us to get busy so he can do something terrible."

"You know, Mrs. Delaney, there's always the possibility that it's not King at all."

"Oh, no. Don't even say it, Sheriff. It's bad enough that you even *think* it. But to actually *say* it out loud the way you did that day—"

"It's just a suggestion."

"Well, it's a terrible suggestion."

Hap had been listening, enjoying the spectacle of his old man trying to be nice to this crazy lady. Now he smirked and said, "I guess I'll go have some coffee."

When Hap was gone, Burrell said, "Have you ever actually *seen* King dig up your roses?"

"You mean with my own eyes?"

He sighed. "Yes, with your own eyes, Mrs. Delaney."

"With my own eyes, no. But I don't need my own eyes to know it's King who's always doing this. You certainly can't be suggesting that my own little Princess could possibly—"

"Little dogs can be just as rambunctious as big dogs, Mrs. Delaney."

"Not Princess," she said, and started to turn away. "And don't think I'm going to forget this. There's an election coming up in November and you have to stand for office." She shook a scolding finger at him. "And I'm going to tell every citizen of this town the kind of terrible things you said about my sweet little Princess."

And with that, she left.

Burrell closed the door and went back to the kitchen table.

He sat down and started finishing off the coffee he'd been working on. He said, "So what did that mean when you said that you weren't the only one who'd better be careful?"

Hap shrugged. "I shouldn't have said that, Pa. I take it back."

"You can't take it back. You already said it."

Hap said, "Just forget it, Pa. All right?"

"I want to know what you meant by it. And I want to know now."

They could both feel his temper getting ready to burst wide again so Hap, very carefully, said, and in not much more than a whisper, "Those clothes you buried in the woods. I know about them, Pa. And I know how careful you have to be about them. That's all I meant."

6

Paul O'Brien was a wheelwright and a successful one. You could tell this with only two quick glimpses. One was the number of wagons, carriages, and coaches that stood on either side of his barn doors waiting to be repaired. And two because, while there were eight men working on various other wagons, carriages, and coaches—men who wore faded, cheap work clothes and had already sweated through them though it was barely midmorning, men who cast nervous eyes in the direction of the boss man whenever he came around— O'Brien himself wore a suit that had been shipped all the way from Kansas City. And he strutted around with his thumbs in the pockets of his vest, like an overseer of slaves. If he ever did much work, he kept it secret.

Hammers pounded, saws cut, axles turned; the not unpleasant odors of oil, sawn lumber, and cured leather for the fancier vehicle seats traveled the soft breezes of the day. In back, a half dozen horses of various breeds and age stood lazily inside a rope corral, watching other animals fly, run, and hop past— birds, dogs, and rabbits mostly.

His royal blondness appeared out back of his shop around ten that morning, stepping smartly to a small black rig that was the latest fashion in rigs. One of his men had attached a sparkling black horse to the rig a few minutes earlier. It was time for his blondness and his wonderfulness to head for town where he'd have midmorning café coffee with the other merchants who, unlike him, actually got work done during the day.

O'Brien was just picking up the reins when Fargo appeared as if by magic, using the single step on the left side of the vehicle to plant himself right next to the boss man.

Fargo angled his Colt in such a way that nobody but O'Brien could see it.

"What the hell is this?" O'Brien said. He had the look of a spoiled and unhappy child. But there was a suggestion of power in his churlishness. "I don't carry much money on me."

"We're going for a ride."

"The hell we are. All I need to do is shout for one of my men."

"You think they can travel faster than a bullet? They'll have to. Because the minute you open your mouth, I'm putting a bullet in your heart."

"You riffraff sonofabitch."

"Let's get going, O'Brien. Take the road there out front to the country."

"I was headed in the opposite direction. Into town."

"Well, then I'm going to break your heart, because we're going into the country."

"You'll never get away with this."

"With what? We're going for a ride, that's all."

"A ride. Highwaymen don't take people for a 'ride.' You're kidnapping me, aren't you?"

"I'd never thought of that, actually. But now that you mention it, maybe it's worth thinking about. The trouble is finding anybody who'd put up ransom money for some punk like you."

"You'll pay for this. Don't you worry about that. You'll pay for this."

"Get going."

O'Brien went on a rant about kidnapping, about all

the important people he knew, about how he'd hire somebody to hunt Fargo down and kill him.

The countryside was gorgeous with the season. It actually *was* a nice day for a ride in the country. Fargo just wished he was in better company was all.

Fargo said, "You finally figured out a way to take care of Curt Cates, huh?"

"I know who you are, Fargo. You're his friend who came here to save him. But it's too late. He'll be dead very soon now."

"There's a good chance you might die before he does."

O'Brien had recovered some of his poise and arrogance. "You kidnap me, hold me for ransom, collect your money—and then what? Beat a confession out of me?"

"You're giving me a lot of good ideas. Keep going."

"None of this'll work, Fargo. He killed her and everybody knows it. You might be able to get some money for me but any confession I sign'll be tossed out. Everybody'll know it was under duress."

"There's somebody you haven't counted on, O'Brien."

"Yeah? And who would that be?"

"Somebody who saw you and the Potter girl together the night she died."

"Bullshit."

"You think so? I'm taking her to the sheriff's office this afternoon."

O'Brien laughed. "You go anywhere near the sheriff's office and somebody'll shoot you on sight. I doubled the reward on you this morning. Somebody's going to get all fast and sassy on your carcass, Fargo."

After listening to the clop of the horse's hooves, and inhaling deeply of the wild flowers that bloomed on the roadsides, Fargo said, "This person'll come forward anyway. Maybe they'll go ahead and kill Cates—maybe they'll even kill me—but that won't stop this person. People'll still have to listen. And even if it's too late, they'll realize that they hanged the wrong man."

"You're making all this up."

"Am I? Think about that night. How dark it was. Weren't you nervous about being out there with the Potter girl?"

"I wasn't nervous because I wasn't there."

"Sure you were. Now tell me about it."

"I wasn't there."

"Pull over here," Fargo said, indicating a wide grassy area around a stand of birch trees.

He pulled over. Fargo could feel his fear.

"What're you going to do?" O'Brien said and for the first time Fargo had the satisfaction of hearing fear in the man's voice.

"This," Fargo said and hit him hard on the side of the head with the handle of his Colt.

Stan Thayer pulled his wagon up to the front yard of the Cates place and reined his horse to a stop. A lot of folks had to worry about kids climbing in and out of their wagons all the time, playing and getting into things. That was one worry Stan Thayer didn't have. Nobody, not even kids, wanted to play in or around a wagon that carried dead people. Stan had a corpse in back now, in fact. Had picked up old Dud Scrimmins on the way out here, the Scrimmins grandson having come to Stan's mortuary to tell him that Gramps had passed on. Apparently he was drunk and got a chicken bone caught in his throat during a family dinner and then got all red and purple in the face and did this crazy dance, his eyes pleading all the time for help and mercy. Nobody knew quite what to do except the oldest boy, Bobby, who kept slamming the old man in the back in hopes that the bone would come flying out of Gramps's throat. But no such luck. So now under the tarp, a jay resting on where his gut was or thereabouts, lay Dud Scrimmins, a man Stan Thayer had never cared much for anyway. Far as Stan knew, the bone was still in the old man's throat. He'd asked Grandma Scrimmins if she wanted him to take the bone out but she said no, not if he'd have to make an incision in the old man's throat. She wanted him to look good for the wake, which she would've held at her place except that they had all them dogs and they pretty much shit an everything so nobody could stand to be anywhere near it.

Serena Cates, a pretty gal if Stan Thayer had ever seen one, came out of the cabin wiping her hands on her apron. He wondered how she'd look naked and then he wondered how she'd look naked and dead. Naked and naked and dead were two different things in his experience, unless you got 'em naked right after they'd passed, when they were still warm. That happened every once in a while.

"Morning, Stan."

"Morning, Serena. Hear you had some excitement here this morning."

She frowned. "Don't take long for word to get around *this* town, does it?"

"Sure don't," Stan said, and there was a sudden woeful tone to his voice. "And it don't matter if it's true or not—what they say, I mean."

Serena's dark eyes reflected the pity most good folks felt for Stan. The bad folks never showed anything remotely like pity. They just gossiped about him. Nobody'd ever seen him with a gal. And what about those mysterious trips he took three, four times a year to Denver? And every once in a while you'd see him giving candy to little kids on the street. If it was anyone else, it might not have even registered, but there was something not right when it came to Stan Thayer.

He always tried to pretend to himself that none of them could hurt his feelings. He had a good amount of money stashed away, his mortuary also provided him with a nice home on the third floor, and he had a lot of creature comforts that nobody but rich folks could afford. Most of the time, he used his money and his home and his creature comforts to hold his loneliness and sorrow at bay—but every once in awhile he'd be unable to hold it off. He wasn't what they whispered he was. Never had a single thought like that in his life. He had a normal interest in children, nothing more. And he liked women just fine. It was just that every time he got around one he might have had designs on—he couldn't talk straight, he just sounded like a fool. And he sweated, oh my Lord did he sweat when he almost got to the point of asking a lady out. But he dreamed of them. In his mind he'd been married a hundred times and sired a couple hundred children. But when he got right up close to it—.

"Sheriff Burrell was out here. It sure mattered to him, seeing his deputy tied up that way."

"I take it your friend Fargo did the tying up?"

She sighed. "He's just trying to prove that my husband's innocent, and so is Fargo."

"That's why I stopped out," Thayer said.

"I don't understand, Stan."

He paused a moment, glancing around as if that pair of nearby chipmunks at the edge of the property's woods might be eavesdropping. "I think I can prove that Curt didn't kill that girl. And that Fargo didn't murder the woman in the hotel."

"My Lord," Serena said. "You're not playing tricks are you, Stan?"

He shook his head. "You got some coffee I could have?"

"You come right inside, Stan Thayer." Her voice was raspy with excitement. "I've got all the coffee you can drink."

* * *

Fargo said, "How's your head?"

"It hurts," O'Brien replied.

"It'll hurt a lot more the second time I hit you."

"You have no right—"

, "I don't need any right. All I need is to keep hitting you over the head till you tell me the truth." Fargo didn't know for sure if O'Brien had actually seen Lilly Potter alone. But there was only one way he was going to find out. After everything Serena Cates had told him about O'Brien, slugging him wasn't all that unpleasant a job, anyway. In fact, come to think of it, he sort of enjoyed it.

He slugged him one more time on the side of the head. But not hard enough to knock him out. He needed O'Brien to talk.

They sat on the wagon seat. O'Brien held his head right after Fargo hit him. Held his head as if it was his child. Held it with great and tender care.

"How many times you see her, O'Brien?"

O'Brien groaned.

Fargo raised his gun, showed it to O'Brien.

O'Brien, looking around at the empty land—looking for somebody to rescue him when there was no hope of rescue at all—said, "Five, maybe six times."

"You have sex with her?"

O'Brien closed his eyes. He was like a tiny tyke who closed his eyes to make things go away. But he wasn't a tiny tyke and neither was Fargo.

"I enjoy hitting you, O'Brien. And if you don't answer my questions, I'll start hitting you all over again."

"A couple of times."

"You had sex with her a couple of times?"

"Yes." Then: "My head's bleeding." He looked with horror at the blood on his hand. He'd been patting his head in different places.

"You trying to make me cry?"

"I'm trying to make you see what you're doing."

"What I'm doing, O'Brien, is trying to get to the truth. Now when was the last time you saw her?"

O'Brien hesitated. "If I tell you, you'll jump to the wrong conclusion."

"When was it?"

"The night she was murdered."

"Why doesn't that surprise me?"

"But I didn't murder her."

"Of course not."

"I don't give a damn if you believe me or not, Fargo."

"You'll give a damn if I hit you again."

O'Brien's voice was thick with self-pity. His collar was red with blood. "I wanted to see her one last time."

"You were breaking it off?"

He started to shake his head. The pain must have been considerable, the way he clutched his temples. "*She* was breaking it off. She said she was in love with somebody else." He hesitated. "She was good sex, Fargo. Very good sex. And I—felt something for her. I surprised myself. The only woman I ever gave a damn about was Serena. But I felt at least *some*thing for Lilly."

"So you killed her and blamed it on Curt Cates."

He started to shake his head again. Stopped. "I won't lie to you, Fargo. There were plenty of times in the past when I'd thought of framing Cates for a murder of some kind. But there was a problem with Lilly."

"Yeah? What kind of problem?"

"I couldn't do it. I—cared about her."

"Who was she in love with?"

"I don't know."

"Guess."

"I honestly don't know. Don't have a clue. And maybe there wasn't anybody at all."

"What's that supposed to mean?"

"The way she talked about this mystery fella. It just didn't sound right somehow. I thought she was making him up as a way of getting rid of me. But then one night—" He stopped talking.

"But then one night what?"

"She sounded—funny. Scared, almost."

"Scared?"

"Yeah. She couldn't seem to concentrate. She was sort of distracted the whole time."

"How was she the night she died?"

"Not scared, if that's what you mean. But she definitely wanted to get rid of me. Said she thought her pa might be following her. That he could be watching her right now. I didn't like the sound of that—her bein' so young and all."

He reached down on the floor of the wagon and picked up his canteen. He groaned as he did so. Apparently, he hadn't figured on his head hurting so much when he bent over. He opened the canteen, poured some water on his hand, and began daubing the water on his face and head. "I could always hire somebody to kill you, you know."

"I reckon you could."

"You hit me again and that's just what I'll do."

Fargo grinned. "Tough guy, huh? Hirin' gunnies is dangerous work."

"Go ahead and make fun, you sonofabitch. I don't give a damn."

"You keep on tellin' me the truth and I won't have any reason to hit you again."

"That mean you believe I didn't frame Cates?"

"It means I think you *probably* didn't. That doesn't mean I'm taking your word as gospel. Or that my mind couldn't be changed if somethin' else came up."

"Well, I didn't frame him. And I don't have any idea who did—I'm not even sure he was framed. You see him like this saint, like he could never bring himself to cheat on Serena. He's a human being like you and me. And Lilly was a damned good looking woman. Nothin' to say that he couldn't've been tempted and just finally gave in."

"Let's head back to town."

"See. You won't even talk about it. What if he *did* kill her, Fargo?"

"I said let's head back to town. And you keep your mouth shut while we're doing it."

Now it was O'Brien's turn to grin. "You don't even want to *think* it, do you, Fargo? And ain't that a kick in the pants? Deep down you know there's at least a possibility he's guilty, don't you?"

"Didn't I tell you to shut up?"

The grin again. Enjoying himself, expansively. "Yeah, Fargo, I guess you did at that."

Tal Boatman rode into town just after noon. Few people greeted him. Tal's reputation as a sour sort made him unpopular with just about everybody who had ever crossed his path. He haggled over prices, interfered with the business of others, and ridiculed any opinion that differed from his. He wasn't a bully, but that was only because he wasn't tough enough to push people around.

As always, he was surprised by how big the town was getting. Stage lines ran constantly now. And the sidewalks, night and day, were usually filled. The mines in the hazy distance worked three eight-hour shifts. And deputies could be seen drifting up and down the streets, aiming to keep things peaceful.

He wanted to see Andy Madden and he didn't have any trouble. Andy sat at the window in the Friendly Café so that he had a view of the street. Tal and Andy shared an interest in birch bark canoes. They saw each other frequently in summer, in and around the river.

Madden gave a curt nod when he saw Tal, leaving the impression—at least in Tal's mind—that Madden didn't want any of the locals to think the two men were good friends. Madden was unpopular enough with certain segments of town folk. He didn't need to be seen putting the grin on Tal Boatman.

Pork, flapjacks, tobacco, coffee—these were the scents that greeted Boatman when he walked into the café and made his way to the window table where Madden sat. A few people looked up at him. None nodded hello.

"You're almost as popular a fella as I am," Madden said.

"I don't give a damn what people think of me."

"Now that's a crock, Tal, and you know it. Just about everybody cares what people think of them. Down deep they do, anyway."

Tal pulled out a chair.

"I don't recall askin' you to sit down," Madden said.

Tal froze in place. He hadn't pulled the chair all the way out. "You're gonna want to hear what I have to say, believe me."

"Oh, yeah? What makes you think that?"

"Because you want to be sheriff someday."

"Now who told you that, Tal? Some saloon drunk shootin' his mouth off?"

"I don't hang out in saloons much, Madden. People don't seem to like me as a drinkin' partner."

Madden grinned. Used his foot to shove Tal's chair all the way out. "That's a sad song, Tal. But I sure hope you got more to say than that."

They didn't talk seriously until the serving woman brought their coffees. Tal said, "This is worse than the dung my sister makes at home."

Madden's smile this time was pure mischief. "You think that might be why people don't like you?"

"Meaning what?"

"Well, you got a sweet little sister and you criticize her just about every time you get a chance. That's somethin' a gentleman ought not to do. In fact, that's somethin' that could get a gentleman knocked on his ass on the wrong night in the wrong place."

"Hell, she's my sister. I got every right to criticize her if I want to. Anyway, that ain't why I came here."

"I'm just sayin', Tal, you say men don't like you as a drinkin' partner. Well, maybe if you wasn't so sour on everybody, maybe they'd like you better."

Tal leaned forward so nobody else could hear but the two of them and said, "What if I could find Skye Fargo for you?"

Tal had expected—wanted—a dramatic jolt to pass through the deputy's body. Something like one of them actor fellas would do on stage when they learned some terrible dark secret. Instead, Madden said, "You're the fourth person inside an hour asked me the same thing."

"Bullshit."

"Bullshit yourself, Tal. You want me to give you the four names?"

When Madden said that, Tal knew he wasn't lying.

Madden said, "That's the problem with rewards. People get so eager, they start seein' things. Convince themselves they see so-and-so practically everywhere they go. And of course they run right to me or the sheriff or one of the other deputies and swear they just seen him and shouldn't that entitle them to part of the reward?"

"Well, I can tell you one thing those other folks can't."

The cool smile. "And just what would that be, Tal?"

"Fargo slept in my barn loft last night."

This time, Tal got the reaction he wanted. Madden sat up straight in his chair and said, "You won't be kiddin' me now, would you Tal?"

But he knew better. Tal wasn't kidding him at all.

7

Fargo spent two hours getting to the Potter homestead. He sat on a hill watching a young woman in gingham bonnet and dress haul water from a creek to a cabin. Then he watched her hang out wash to dry on a single line that stretched from the rear wall of the cabin to a pole about fifteen feet away. He satisfied himself as much as possible that the woman was alone here. He assumed this was Barb Potter.

He drifted down through buffalo grass to the creek where he ground-tied his stallion. He waited until the woman came out of the cabin again. She was headed to the creek with another big pile of laundry to wash in the creek. He hid below the steep clay cliff, hunched down.

He greeted her. "Nice day for working outside."

If she was afraid, she didn't show it. "And who might you be, stranger?" There was accusation in her voice and eyes. She had a doll-like face with blond bangs. She was a bit on the plump side, but fetchingly so.

"I want to talk about your sister."

"You're not law, are you?"

"No, ma'am, I'm not."

"In fact, you're the man the law is *looking* for, aren't you?"

"I'm afraid you're right. They're looking for me. But I didn't kill that girl in the hotel."

"Sure," she said, "just like your friend Curt Cates didn't kill my sister, Lilly."

"I don't believe he did, ma'am, or I wouldn't be trying to help him." But then he remembered what O'Brien had said. How could he be sure Curt hadn't killed her? Men were capable of a lot of things even their best friends didn't know sometimes.

"You don't sound real sure about that."

"I look at it this way, ma'am. The girl in the hotel was killed because she knew who killed your sister. That was why she contacted me. The only person who had any reason to kill her was the same person who killed your sister. Doesn't that follow?"

He could see that he'd at least gotten her interest. "I suppose you could be right."

"Here," he said, "let me give you a hand."

"You going to help me wash the clothes, are you?" She said this with a hint of amusement.

"I'd be willing to bet that I've had a lot worse jobs."

She had a tub and a washboard set up along the creek. She set down her laundry. "You really going to help me?"

"Sure."

"What if I don't talk to you?"

"I'll take my chances."

"You want Cates free. I want him hanged."

"Fair enough. You know where I stand, I know where you stand."

They set about washing the load of dark, heavy clothes. They took turns with the washboard. She soaked the clothes and he wrung them out. It wasn't easy or rewarding work. Like many pioneer tasks, it was dull and spirit-deadening. But that was part of what you had to endure on the frontier. It wasn't just the hard work—it was the sheer number of seemingly insignificant but overwhelming minor tasks you had to do to simply survive. That was why a lot of the people who came west didn't stay long. As one newspaperman had once put it, *A pioneer needs a strong back, a strong head, and a strong soul.*

After a time, he said, "I'm sorry your sister's dead."

"You don't have to get on my good side, mister. She didn't mean anything to you and you know it."

"You think I take pleasure in seeing a young woman die? I'm not that kind, ma'am, whatever else you might think of me."

"She was a whore."

He wasn't sure what to say.

"She carried on with at least half a dozen married men in town over the last four years. She always told me that married men were more fun because it was more dangerous. Sneaking around and everything. You imagine being that brazen? But that's how she was. She sure wasn't raised that way. Ma and Pa raised us both on the Bible. And you know what the Bible says about adultery."

"Is this your Ma and Pa's place?"

"It was. They died in a flood six years ago. Then me and my husband took it over."

"Your husband around now?"

She shook her head. "Thrown by a horse. Everybody told him not to ride that horse but he wouldn't listen. Smashed his head in when he got thrown."

"You sound mad about it."

She'd been working on the ribs of the washboard. She stopped, wiped sweat from her brow with the sleeve of her faded dress. "I lost my folks, my little sister turned into a whore, and I married a man that didn't have a lick of common sense. You'd be mad, too—because what it amounted to was that I was left alone on this homestead—alone, mister. And I don't like it."

"You're a pretty woman. I'm sure you've had men call on you."

She cocked an eyebrow. "You know the one thing I hate more than being alone?"

"I think I can guess."

"If you guess men then you're right."

He wrung out a shirt and said, "Maybe not all men are like your husband."

"I suppose you're not?"

He could feel his stomach and groin tighten with need as she made her question into a kind of challenge. She even stepped close enough to him so that he could feel the tips of her breasts. She knew the power she had over him at this moment. A knowing smile revealed that to him.

Then she was in his arms, as urgently needy as he was. They embraced with a fury that was almost violent and then eased themselves down to the bank.

She wore no underclothes. She was out of her dress in moments, turning and offering her erotic rump to Fargo, who knew just what she wanted.

Her muscles contracted and made his passage even more pleasurable as he entered her. Her buttocks were like creatures unto themselves, shifting, pleasingly soft, thrusting and thrusting and thrusting against him until he had to start pacing himself to last as long as she'd want him to. His hands found their way up under her chest where his palms were filled with her bountiful breasts. He pinched her erect nipples and her hips ground against him even harder. He sensed that she was one of those women who could find their pleasure in intercourse alone.

But she also proved to be one of those women who enjoyed varying the pace and position of the fun. She eased herself away from him and then lay back against the bank.

She grabbed his spear before he could enter her and guided it between her huge, soft breasts where she began pleasuring him by rubbing the tip of his sex with her nipples while she stroked him with her hand.

She sure knew what she was doing. Fargo thought he was going to go blind with pure, unadulterated pleasure.

Then she fooled him again. Just when he thought she was going to let him finish between her breasts, she grabbed his stout rod and lowered it so that he could get inside her. Again, as he thrust himself into her, she tightened the passage for him, using this moment to start groping and using his buttocks as he'd used hers. They were intermingled moisture, heat, and randy thrusting now, almost one in a literal sense as he went ever deeper and she began to use his backside the way the most expert whores did.

She was approaching a climax—this must have been her fourth or fifth—by the time Fargo reached his own soaring fulfillment.

Then there was just the sound of the wind and the water and their own gasping breath.

She laughed. "I guess maybe you could change my mind about men, after all."

After a time, they got dressed and went back to work.

They didn't speak for another fifteen minutes. Certain muscles in his hands were getting tired. Next time he heard a man talk about how "easy" women had it, Fargo would set him straight. Of course, given his vanity, he wouldn't mention that he'd been doing laundry. That wasn't exactly the way to keep your rep as a tough guy. *He's fast on the draw and you should see him do a basket of laundry.*

Horses.

Fargo reached for his Colt.

He put them just about at the cabin. No doubt a posse eager to earn some money by bringing him back.

"Barb! Barb Potter!"

The male voice was stark with youth and urgency.

"Damn Tim Farraday, anyway," she said.

"Who's he?"

She shook her head. "This nineteen-year-old who's been after me since my husband died. He told me yesterday he was going to get up a posse. Sounds like he has. I'd better get up there."

He grabbed her wrist. "I guess I'll have to trust you."

She jerked her hand away. "I guess you'll have to at that, won't you?" Then her expression softened. "Don't worry. I wouldn't turn you over to a bunch of maniacs like Farraday and his friends. They always want to lynch somebody."

The stabbing headache. A moment of darkness filling his eyes. His identity seeming to be at the far, far end of a long, echoing corridor.

"You all right?"

He nodded. "They might see my horse," he said, finally, recovering his focus.

"I'll hide it around back. Don't worry."

She was gone for fifteen minutes. He thought of working himself up to the edge of the cliff and seeing what he could see. Could he really trust her? Maybe she was like her sister, devious. Maybe right now they were quietly sweeping up through the grass, fanning out, to grab him, to make escape impossible. And if they were prone to lynching anyway—how would he stop them? He was too weak for that. He needed to rest. If a posse came for him now, he wouldn't be able to defend himself. Still weak from the attack that had stolen his memories from him, his wounds were both physical and psychological. In combination, they were devastating.

His name was Skye Fargo . . . because they told him so. He was a roughneck adventurer of some kind . . . because they told him so. He had come here to help a man who'd saved his life . . . because they told him so.

The only thing he knew firsthand was that he'd awakened on the floor of a hotel room with a dead girl under the bed. The law thought he'd killed her. They were chasing him. Their reward was such that just about any damn fool would try to bring him in.

Skye Fargo . . . the Trailsman . . . he tried to make some kind of emotional connection between these words and himself. He could understand the words . . . and believed they applied to him . . . but he couldn't *feel* the truth and rightness of them . . .

. . . dreaming . . . a younger version of himself . . . a fishing hole . . . a campfire in the background . . . just waiting for a nice big perch to fry in a pan now that the end of this chill autumn day was drawing nigh.

In the dream there was no doubt he was Skye Fargo. The Trailsman. In the dream he was enjoying one of his rare moments of true peace. Everything was fine . . .

A cool hand on his hot forehead.

The riverbank faded. As did the campfire.

The cool hand on the hot forehead was here and now.

He opened his eyes. The hand belonged to Barb Potter.

"They're gone."

At first he wasn't sure what she was talking about. A jumble of thoughts. Who were "they" exactly? And what was the significance of them being gone?

Then he remembered. Somebody named Farraday. A lynch mob.

"I told you you could trust me."

"Hard to trust anybody these days," he said, his voice startling even to himself—so damned weak. So unlike him.

"You need more rest and more food. They won't be back until at least nightfall. You should be stronger by then."

"What happened to me?"

"You passed out. That's the trouble with head injuries. You think you're all right but you're not. You

74

shouldn't be riding around the countryside, you should be resting up. The sooner you rest, the sooner you'll start feeling strong again. Right now the best you can do is feel strong for a little while at a time."

"I guess you're right there."

"C'mon now. I'll give you a hand and we'll go back to the cabin."

"That sounds awful good about now."

"Home cooking and a good, clean bed."

"That sounds even better. You sure your friends are gone?"

"They're not my friends. But yes, they're gone."

"I really owe you for all this."

"You don't owe me anything. Maybe Cates didn't kill Lilly, after all. That's something I have to face. Same as you have to face the possibility that he *did* kill Lilly. But we can talk after you've had a good meal and some sleep."

She was all pioneer woman. She fought against anything getting her down, fought against her natural inclination to despair from time to time. She was never falsely cheery but she remained optimistic about things. Some hard work . . . some prayers . . . a little bit of luck . . . you'd be surprised at what you could accomplish.

The pioneer spirit.

She got her shoulder under his and helped him up the embankment. It was trial and error. They'd go a couple of steps then slide backward. But she was determined . . .

Farraday and his three friends waited there for them. Guns drawn.

"Well, I'll be damned," Farraday said, an ironic smile on his boyish face. "And here you said you hadn't seen him and were all alone. The way you carry on, a fella might not think he could trust you, Barb. Now that's a hell of a thing, ain't it, a fella like me not bein' able to trust a gal like you?"

75

Fargo had the sense that his life would soon be ended. . . .

Farraday slid off his horse, holstered his gun, and walked to where Barb was holding up Fargo. "You better let me help you with him."

"Don't touch him, Tim, or I swear to God I'll kill you."

A smirk. "Well, well, what have we here? If I didn't know better, I'd say you and this here killer was a pair of lovers, you gettin' all hot and bothered when I just offer to help you out a little."

"You heard what I said, Tim. Get off my land."

" 'Fraid I can't do that, ma'am," Farraday said. "I'm part of a sworn posse lookin' for a fugitive named Fargo. And I do believe I just found him."

Rage was a funny thing, Fargo knew. Even when your strength was gone, even when you could barely form a clear thought, if you hated somebody enough, you found sudden, overwhelming strength. It might only last a moment or two, this kind of strength, but by God it was there if you wanted it.

It was there and Fargo wanted it.

He'd had enough of this town and all of its punks of various ages. His friend was going to be hanged for a murder he didn't commit, and now he looked to share the same fate. Well, there was one thing he knew for sure and they were going to learn it, too—the hard way. To get him to the gallows, they were going to have to fight the maddest man this side of the Mississippi.

He hurled himself into a stunned Farraday, smashing fists into his face, his throat, his chest, his sternum, and his belly before Farraday could raise a single hand in response. His two cronies shouted oaths and curses. One of them took his gun out. But he sure as hell couldn't shoot into this blur of flying fists and tumbling bodies without endangering Farraday's life. He put the pistol back in the holster. And neither man wanted to get tangled up in the brawl. This Fargo—who just a minute ago had looked so pale and exhausted that he could barely stand up even with Barb Potter supporting him—he'd turned into some kind of murderous whirling dervish. If he wasn't pounding on Farraday, he was kicking him; if he wasn't kicking him, he was head-butting him. He seemed crazed, like a man who had suddenly lost all sense and reason and was some kind of animal that could be brought down only by a fusillade of gunfire.

Farraday ended up on his back, his face bloody. Unconscious.

Fargo picked him up, carried him to his horse and flung him across his saddle. The others had been so absorbed in the battle they hadn't seen Fargo toss Barb his Colt in the middle of the beating. She held it on them now, steady.

"Get off my land," she said, "right after you throw your guns down. And I mean your rifles, too."

"Aw, Barb, c'mon," one of the men said. "I just got this here rifle for my birthday."

"I wouldn't mind shooting you, Ned," she said. "Ever since you got me under the blanket at the church picnic that time and put your hands all over me."

"Hell, Barb, that was ten years ago," he whined. "I was only twelve."

"It doesn't matter. I asked you to stop and you didn't. So I'm not gonna get worried about your birthday rifle. Throw it down on the ground."

"You sure do hold a grudge," the man said.

"Yeah, and you'd better remind your friend Farraday of that, too, when he wakes up. Tell him next time he sets foot on my land, I'll put a bullet through his forehead."

The two men looked at each other. Even though she wasn't throwing punches, this little gal seemed every bit as mad and crazed as Fargo had.

"Now get goin'," she said.

The man who'd felt her up at the church picnic a decade previous—and she sure did hold a grudge—grabbed the reins of Farraday's horse and led the animal away. He was still shaking his head over the whole incident. A man goes out to apprehend a fugitive and look what he gets. He sees the toughest young man in town get his head kicked in, and then on top of that, she has to bring up something that happened ten damned years ago. Riding posse used to be a whole lot easier. A man didn't get hisself humiliated by a well-built little gal with a gun.

Fargo was spent.

He let her drag him to the creek, soak his face and head in an attempt to bring him back to strength.

"You need to get out of here, Skye. They'll be back with half the town and they'll shoot you on sight." She smiled. "You're a pretty terrifying man when you get mad."

"I can't take getting pushed around anymore."

"This town has that effect on people."

"Your sister have any special friends?"

She thought a moment. "A girl named Veronica Day. A very religious girl, believe it or not. They were friends a long time. Lilly even thought of joining their sect when she was young. But then Lilly got sort of wild and they had a falling out. It was funny, though."

"What was?"

"The last couple months of her life—Lilly started riding out to the Day homestead. Seeing Veronica again."

"You know why?"

"I'm not sure. Lilly was kind of strange lately. I think she got pretty tired of the life she was leading."

"She say that to you?"

"No, but I sensed it." She laughed. "Lilly wouldn't want to give her older sister the satisfaction of seeing that she'd been right. I'd told Lilly that she'd get sick

78

of the life she was leading. But she'd only tell that to Veronica."

"Sounds like she might be worth a visit."

"You doing all right? Your memory and everything?"

He touched his head. "I get so I don't even think about it for a while. I just go on with everything. But then it'll hit me—I still don't know who the hell I am. I only know who people *tell* me I am. If I could remember—I got a glimpse of the person who knocked me out in that hotel room—I know I did. If I could remember—"

"You need to get out of here, Skye. And fast."

Fargo climbed up on his horse. "Thanks for everything. Maybe I'll see you again."

"You make a *point* of seeing me again." She smiled. "Or else."

"I forgot. You hold grudges."

She touched his knee. "You damned right I do, Skye, and don't you forget it. Now get out of here before they come back."

Sheriff Henry Burrell couldn't seem to get much done. Every time he'd start to concentrate on some piece of business, his mind would be jolted back to the conversation he'd had with his son.

The bloody and buried clothes.

How the hell had Hap found out about them? And more important, what was he going to do about them?

He'd half-expected Hap to stop in during the day, maybe suggest they go over to the café and have a cup of coffee and piece of apple pie the way they sometimes did.

But there'd been no sign of Hap and it was already pushing on toward two o'clock in the afternoon.

He'd have to dig up the clothes and move them. But that would be the easy part.

Dealing with Hap would be a whole lot harder.

*   *   *

The first thing Tal Boatman did wrong was to bring Maya Boatman a chocolate bar. The second thing he did wrong was to offer to help her with her chores. And the third thing he did wrong was to compliment her on her cooking, which he did while he scarfed down a chunk of beef and a piece of bread.

She said, "What're you up to, Tal?"

"Up to? Who said I was 'up to' anything?"

"Chocolate. Chores. Compliments. You want something."

"Now there's a hell of a note," he said sardonically, sitting at the table across from where she sat in the rocking chair with her knitting. You wouldn't think a blind girl could knit. But she'd carefully taught herself how to do it over the years. She wasn't about to win prizes at the county fair—some of that knitting was so elaborate, a person had to wonder if it hadn't been worked up by some kind of magician—but she did a workmanlike job with only a few mistakes here and there. "You all the time complain that I'm not very nice to you. And so I'm nice to you and now you complain about that. You sure do get confusing sometimes, Sis."

"I still say you want something."

"I do."

"There. See? I knew it."

"I want my sister to feel safe and happy and know that I love her very much."

She laughed. It was cute, a sort of giggle-laugh. "Oh, Lord, when you put on the butter you go all the way, don't you? I'm surprised you could even say those things without laughing out loud."

"Go ahead. Make fun. I guess you don't care about my feelings much, do you?"

"Oh, c'mon, Tal." She giggled again. "Just tell me what you want and spare me all the butter, all right?"

Tal decided the best thing now was to probably say

it straight out, after a little build-up to demonstrate that what he was proposing made sense.

"I don't have to tell you about the well, do I?"

"You sure don't. We need somebody to come out and look at it."

"Or the roof."

"We need a new roof. There's no doubt about that."

Tal couldn't believe how easy this was going to be. He'd mention a few more things that badly needed fixing around here and then he'd just sort of slip in, *And we can have all these things just by turning Fargo over to the Deputy and we'll get the reward. We'll get everything fixed up nice and fine and still have a lot of money left over.*

"Did I mention the wagon? We could sure use a new axle."

"You didn't mention the wagon—or the plow or the things we need for winter." She paused. "But it won't work."

"Huh?"

"Even if I knew where Fargo was, I wouldn't tell you. He didn't murder that girl, Tal, and I'm sure not going to help Sheriff Burrell and his deputies get their hands on him. New roof or not."

"You stupid bitch!" he snapped and slammed out of the house. Outside, he faced the house and shouted again, "You blind, stupid bitch! You'll be damned sorry you didn't help me!"

She had to smile to herself. There wasn't much else she could do. *I want my sister to feel safe and happy and know that I love her very much.*

Nobody could spread on the butter like her dear, sweet brother Tal.

An hour later, Fargo came up over a rise and fell face first off his horse. The hurt and the exhaustion were back on him.

He lay in a state that was not quite sleep, yet not quite wakefulness for more than half an hour. Then he managed to summon enough strength to crawl to a copse of pines and lie down again.

The area was heavily wooded with narrow strips of pasture separating the various patches of forest.

He had a nightmare about being lynched. Sweat beads the size of rubies stood out on his unshaven face. A noose bit into his neck, drawing blood it was so coarse. A crowd of dead people with leprosy pocking and disfiguring their corpses stood all around him, toothless grins on their blood-dripping mouths.

When he finally woke again, a late-afternoon breeze tousled his hair and rose goosebumps on his arms.

A tiny, female voice said, "I ought to blast you right now and never even tell Pa about you."

A continuation of the nightmare? That happened sometimes, didn't it? You slipped out of one nightmare, thinking it was over, only to find yourself trapped in another one.

If this was a nightmare . . .

She was maybe twelve, thirteen. She wore the dark bonnet and dress of a strict religious sect. The difference was she held a rifle that was practically as long as she was pointed directly at Fargo.

"You killed Nan. You're the bad man they're looking for."

"Who're you?"

"I'm Darcy Miller. And you're the man who killed my big sister." She hesitated. "At least that's what they say."

"You have doubts about it?" Fargo struggled to smile. There was a sweet tentativeness about the young girl he liked. Maybe it was nothing more than fear of a stranger. But for whatever reason, she obviously had some doubts about him being the killer of her sister.

"I didn't kill her, Darcy."

"You don't have the kind of face I thought you would."

"What kind of face did you *think* I'd have?"

"Oh, you know. Like a wanted poster. You know how them men look. They look crazy. I seen some wanted posters once and they gave me nightmares for a week."

"Get on your feet," said an angry male voice.

The man had just appeared over a slope in the hill behind Darcy. He resembled the kind of nightmare creature Darcy had been describing.

Fargo's first squint-eyed impression of the man was that he was the most unruly, unkempt, bad-smelling giant he'd ever seen. He wore buckskin—shirt, leggings, moccasins—and he carried a rifle identical to Darcy's. The white beard was what grabbed your attention, though. The damned thing stretched from his nostrils to his belt and was half as wide as the considerable span of his shoulders. And it was tangled as a briar patch, stubbled and knotty with what appeared to be encrusted food, drink, and even pieces of foliage here and there. It almost looked as if this—thing—had been decorated this way on purpose.

Then there was the smell. Take an outhouse on a windless 100-degree afternoon. Take a slaughterhouse at its busiest. Take an animal that was being consumed by buzzards and maggots. Put them all together and you had some small sense of what the man stank like. And he was still many feet away from Fargo.

If Darcy noticed the smell, she didn't let on.

"This is him, Pa."

"I know, girl. We'll take him back to the root cellar."

"We gonna skin him, Pa?"

"Not quite yet."

"We gonna burn him?"

"I need to think, girl, now hush."

"You going to set them rattlers on him?"

"Did you hear me, girl? I said 'hush'."

She finally hushed.

"You ain't got up yet."

"You going to arrest me?" Fargo said.

"That'll come in its own good time."

"I want to be taken to the sheriff's office." Skinning him, burning him, and setting rattlers on him made the notion of a jail cell sound awfully inviting.

"You're mighty choosy for a man I got a gun on."

Looking at this odd, startling creature—he was part man, part forest beast—made Fargo realize that there were worse ways to go than lynching. At least most lynch mobs took baths once in a while. And didn't have beards that displayed the last few months of their dinners. And God knew what else.

It happened quickly. The man stepped forward and used the butt of his rifle as a club. He smashed it against Fargo's head twice—and that was it.

Dark, dank, cold when Fargo awoke. There was the moment when he could not form a single coherent thought as to who he was, where he was, or why his head hurt so much. There was the moment when he tried to stand but fell right back down. And there was the moment when it all came flooding back.

My name is Skye Fargo. Some tinhorn sonofabitch of a sheriff says I murdered a girl in a hotel room. I've been running ever since. There's a reward for me. A gal says I'm Skye Fargo and she wouldn't have any reason to lie to me. She said I came to town here to help save her husband's life as he once helped me save mine. Some strange little girl got a rifle on me and then her mountain-beast of an old man threw down on me, too. She mentioned a root cellar. This is it—or else this is a grave and I just haven't realized it yet.

There was more information. He remembered what Serena Cates had told him about himself, how she'd filled in some of the bigger blanks. But now—on his own—he was starting to fill in blanks on his own. Childhood memories. Young man memories. People, places, events.

He was Skye Fargo. And he didn't need to be *told* that anymore. He knew it. Knew it in his mind and knew it in his gut. In fact, many of the memories were quite recent. He pictured himself riding into town here. Meeting with Curt in jail. Meeting with Serena. Meeting with half a dozen people, trying to prove that Curt wasn't a killer.

He remembered everything right up to going to the hotel and starting inside the door and then—

The same sort of darkness he was trapped in now, though he didn't remember the darkness of the hotel room being gravelike.

He stumbled to his feet. Damn, his head was so painful and so fragile he had an image of it tumbling off his shoulders. The mountain-beast must have really hit him with that rifle of his.

He thought of the blind girl he'd met. Maya Boatman. Her whole life was lived this way, poor sweet girl. This darkness.

He prowled around the perimeter of the large root cellar, feeling the various vegetables and other foodstuffs that had been stored here. The dirt of the wall and floor were equally coarse and in the chill of the place he could sense tiny nocturnal creatures moving about. Some of them would be as common as worms. Some of them would be exotic. Them, he'd rather not think about.

Then he found the rungs. A ladder. Wooden. When he looked straight up he could see the vague outline of a trap door. Daylight or lamplight, he couldn't tell which for sure, outlining the square door.

If he was ever to get away from here, this would be the only path available to him.

He grasped the ladder. Wobbly. He put a foot on the lowest rung. It felt weak, or maybe it was just him.

The wood had no doubt started to deteriorate over the years in the dank climate.

He started working his way up, pausing every few rungs to make sure nobody above could hear him. The closer he got to the trapdoor above, the louder two or three voices became. But he couldn't hear any words clearly. Just the ominous rumbling tone of the father and the bright tone of the little girl.

He had just reached the top of the ladder when he heard the front door slam. They'd gone out. Somewhere a dog barked. Apparently out in the yard. Then a silence that only made him seem all the more isolated. His entire reality was the chill gravelike darkness in which he'd awakened.

He began trying to push the door upward. Since one hand was not strong enough to smash the door open, he tried both hands, and damned near took the ladder tumbling down with him. He'd been so desperate to get out, he'd lost common sense. A ladder as rickety as this one required tight handling. With both his hands on the bottom of the trap door, the ladder tended to lean backward. He couldn't afford a fall that would break an arm or a leg.

He heard a distant shot.

While they'd taken his Colt, they hadn't searched him entirely. He found his Arkansas Toothpick sheathed against his ankle. He worked it up into the outline of the door, trying to find where the latch was. Maybe it would be a simple latch. One he could open from here.

He worked so feverishly that, despite the chill of the root cellar, beads of sweat rolled down his forehead and stung his eyes. He worked his blade around the entire trapdoor but wasn't able to find the latching mechanism, whatever it might be. The blade wasn't long enough. They'd built the trapdoor several inches deep.

They came back. The front door was slammed open,

the dog went into ecstasy, and the little girl said, loud and clear, "That's the biggest possum you ever shot, Pa."

"I'm gonna fix him up real good. You'n your brother're gonna have a feast tonight, believe me."

"We gonna give him some?"

"Give who some, girl?"

"The man in the cellar."

A boy's voice, then. Older than the girl. In his teens. He laughed. "I bet I know what Pa's gonna give him. He's gonna give him that satchel of rattlers he's got in the snake pit, ain'tcha, Pa? You remember how that last one screamed, Darcy? That fat man, Pa took all his money? He screamed real, real good."

"But the good book don't say to treat strangers like that, Smiley Bill."

"The good book," Smiley Bill scoffed, "sure don't say be nice to strangers if'n they was the ones what killed your own flesh and blood."

"You help get the skillet ready, Darcy," Pa said. "I'll be preparin' the possum."

There wasn't much to do now except retreat back to the ground floor. Fargo kept thinking of the young girl, Darcy. She obviously felt some kind of sympathy for him.

When he'd found the Toothpick, he'd also found some lucifers in his pocket. He decided to burn two of them now, get a better look at the root cellar. That would leave him with three.

The first match revealed little that was unexpected. Couple of dusty shelves with dusty jars of vegetables so old they resembled baby monsters rather than edible foodstuffs. The kind of thing you saw in circuses and pawned off as monsters. A rickety chair, a pile of magazines, and then, when he toed a box aside, he saw—

—and then the match burned out.

Just when he thought he'd seen—

He struck the second Lucifer and confirmed what his first glimpse had only hinted at. A pile of bones—and clearly human bones—that reached halfway up the wall. At one time, the bones must have formed the architectural structure of six or seven human beings.

He remembered what Darcy had said about the good book telling you to be kind to strangers. The crazed mountain man obviously had his own way of dealing with them, one the good book would not approve of at all.

Then, in the last moments of the flickering flame, he saw the remnants of the rattlers. They'd died down here, too, along with the people they'd poisoned. Not their fault. They were snakes and they'd done what snakes do. The people had probably died horrible deaths. He remembered something the little girl had said to her Pa. About eating them. Cannibalism certainly wasn't unheard of on the frontier. But it was certainly frowned upon. This almost made Fargo smile, the thought of Pa giving a damn what anybody thought of him. Pa was Pa, a law unto himself.

The rotting snakeskins still had a bit of shimmer to them. Then the match burned out.

Fargo thought of lighting another match, looking around even more. But no, he might need the other matches.

Darkness. Cold. A sense of disorientation.

He went through his litany of Skye Fargo attributes. A brave man. A man who helped the needy, needy being somebody who needed the price of a meal or a bully removed from his back. The Trailsman, they called this man.

Him.

Skye Fargo *did* have to smile this time. If the Trailsman helped out the needy . . . he was in dire need of helping himself out now.

But how was he going to do it when he couldn't get

the trap door open—the trap door that represented the only possible way out of this hellish hole?

He listened as feet tromped across the floor above him. The front door opening and closing. Fading voices of son and father.

And after a time, the sweet young voice of Darcy singing a mountain song of lost love that moved Fargo more than he would have expected. The melancholy of the song was not unlike his own melancholy. The song told of a young man spurned by his woman and doomed to wander the hills in search of a new love. As Fargo searched for his identity, he could be told a thousand times who he was, but he still had to feel it, believe it for himself.

He realized then that Darcy might help him. She might listen to his story. See that he wasn't the badman she thought. It was likely his only hope. And if she didn't help him . . .

If she didn't help him, God alone knew how he was going to get out of this gravelike cellar. . . .

8

Around two that afternoon, Sheriff Henry Burrell told his deputies to watch over the office, that he was "slipping home" for the rest of the day. They took turns spelling each other in this fashion. It was democratic. They rotated the privilege of "slipping home" when there wasn't much going on at the office. Four of them, Burrell and his deputies, rotating the privilege.

He might as well go home, he thought, as he rode his roan down the dusty road. He couldn't think of anything except his son Hap finding those bloody clothes. He wondered where Hap was now. Probably getting liquored up somewhere. When he was drunk, he often belittled Burrell about how pathetic it was to be a lawman in a town like this one. If he had any guts or gumption, Hap always implied, he'd be toting a badge in a much bigger town. All this criticism from a punk who couldn't—or wouldn't—hold a job. There was no heartbreak like the heartbreak of having a child whose behavior humiliated you at every turn—whose behavior marked you as a softheaded fool who couldn't control your own flesh and blood.

He unsaddled his horse, fed him, brushed him, and then headed for the woods, toting a shovel he'd grabbed from the barn. He'd seen no sign of Hap. Again, he assumed he'd find his son—if he bothered himself to look—in some saloon somewhere. No doubt playing cards. The day was gently warm, with soft breezes penetrating even the deep confines of the forest. A day for fishing or just simply loafing. Not a day for digging up bloody clothes.

A couple of times, he felt panic when he couldn't find the hole he'd dug. His mind was so knotted up with thoughts of Hap—dark thoughts; dangerous thoughts—that he couldn't think clearly. But then with the help of some chittering squirrels and a rather somber-looking raccoon—a big fella—he saw a clear patch where the earth had recently been disturbed. He set to work.

The clothes were gone.

He sat down, weary beyond his years, on the gnarled limb that lightning had ripped from its tree. He rolled himself a cigarette and let the work-sweat on his body dry from the breeze.

He'd assumed that Hap would have left the clothes where he'd found them. This would be sufficient to get from his old man the things he wanted. Namely, cash. Over the past three years, Hap had gotten himself into several scrapes with various professional gamblers in the area. He'd paid off his debt in various ways. He'd won a little back at cards but mostly he'd stolen—from his father, from a few merchants in the deep of night, and at least one time in a stagecoach stickup. The kind of gamblers who were after Hap for bad debts didn't give a damn that the young man's father was the law. One way or the other, they wanted their money. They'd kill Hap if necessary—it would only enhance their reputations for ruthlessness—and worry about Henry Burrell later. They could always leave the area if necessary and pick up their trade somewhere else. That was the nice thing about gambling. Anywhere you went, you had men and women eager to have their hard-earned money taken from them.

Burrell filled in the hole again, tamped it down, disguised it with as much foliage as he could find. He'd probably never come back here. What was the point, with Hap in possession of the bloody clothes?

He headed back to his house. He walked slowly. He was afraid of what he might do if he saw Hap. He was just glad his wife hadn't lived to see how Hap had turned out.

Some folks argued that a broken heart couldn't kill you. Maybe not—leastways in the way of a romantically broken heart. But a misbehaving kid—a drunk, a gambler, a bully, a kid who survived in part because his old man was the law—this was the kind of kid who could kill you through sheer heartbreak. You could only take so much before your will to live began to drain out of you. Then death began to look like a blessing.

Hap's horse was there.

The confrontation he'd been dreading was here at last.

He went to the back door and let himself inside. Hap sat at the only table they had. A whiskey bottle sat in front of him. A cigarette was tucked into the corner of his mouth. The bloody clothes sat in the middle of the table.

"You looking for these, were you?"

Burrell sat down. Grabbed the whiskey bottle. Took two swigs for himself and then set the bottle down hard.

"What the hell's all this about?"

"It's about Paul Iverson. I owe him four thousand dollars."

"Oh, God, Hap, why'd you ever have to play cards with him? He probably dealt you off the bottom."

"Well, he sure did something," Hap said, frowning, "because he won every hand."

"And you had to keep betting."

"The only way I could get my money back."

"So what do you want me to do about it, Hap?"

Hap touched the bloody clothes balled up on the table. "I need to get some money and get out of this territory and never come back."

"And just how the hell're you going to get that kind of money?"

"The bank." Hap smiled. "You're going to help me rob it."

When the trapdoor was lifted, Fargo sprang from sleep. He'd tucked himself in the corner, trying to stay warm in the dark tomb of the root cellar.

He was on his feet. Moving swiftly to the ladder. He looked up at the open trapdoor. He had a sensation of light, warmth. Every ounce of him wanted to be up there in that light and warmth. He knew better than to start up the ladder. Anybody who wanted to could just push it away from the foot-long space between the ladder's top and the trapdoor. He'd be flung backward to the floor many feet below. He didn't need any more injuries.

A lantern appeared at the top of the open door suddenly and young Darcy peeked her head down. "You don't tell my Pa I did this or he'll beat us both."

"Tell him what, Darcy?"

"This."

She dropped something small and square wrapped in paper.

He caught it.

"There's bread and some beef."

"Thank you."

"And this. But you'll have to hide it somewhere when they come down."

A blanket. Tattered, thin, stained. But it would provide at least a bit of warmth.

"How come you're doing this?"

" 'Cause you're one of God's creatures. And that's what the good book says I *should* do. The way Pa reads the Bible is all wrong. All he sees in it is punishment for sinners. And like the book says, we're *all* sinners."

He smiled. "Somehow I doubt you are, Darcy."

"Oh, I have terrible thoughts sometimes."

"You do? You're too sweet to have terrible thoughts. How old are you?"

"Twelve. And when Pa's beating me, I have plenty of terrible thoughts. One time, I even thought of waiting till he was asleep and then taking his pistol and killing him right there in his sleep. That's about as terrible a thought as you can have, mister."

"We all have thoughts like that, Darcy. Especially when somebody's beating us."

She hesitated. "And then I have thoughts of running away. Like Nan did. But I wouldn't become a whore. I'd just run away somewhere where it was nice and peaceful and where people read the Bible the right way."

Fargo knew he was about to use her to his own ends. But it was the only way he might ever get out of here. And he'd certainly be doing her a favor.

"That's what I need to do, Darcy. Run away from here. As soon as I can. I'd be happy to take you with me."

She didn't have time to answer. They both heard the same sounds at the same time. Father and son talking as they approached the front door.

The lantern was pulled up. The trapdoor was eased down, shut.

Darkness again.

He took food and blanket to the rickety chair he'd seen. He wrapped the blanket around him and began to pull on the tough beef. The bread was fresh and satisfying. Especially the crust.

He allowed himself the fantasy of escape. Darcy'd come back at the next opportunity and they'd run away together. He'd find a good home for her and then he'd resume his search for the killer. He realized for the first time since being abandoned down here that Curt Cates had less than twenty-four hours to live if Fargo didn't come up with the real killer.

So far, all he knew was that he didn't know much at all. Almost everybody he'd met seemed suspicious for one reason or another. And there was always the possibility—much as he didn't want to consider it— that Curt himself had murdered the girl. Fargo didn't think so—but he couldn't dismiss it, either.

The cry came soon after he finished his humble meal.

The crack of a strong hand on bone and then the cry. Easy—too easy—to picture. Good ole Pa slapping his daughter. Hard.

"That lantern's hot, girl. That means you lit it. Now why would you light it when the sun's still full up?"

"I didn't light it, Pa. It must still be hot from last night."

She wasn't much of a liar. She sounded desperate.

Another resounding, echoing slap. Followed by a crash. He must have knocked her over something. Another cry.

Pa had apparently lost his mind again. "You're gonna get the belt! You took that lantern and went down there, didn't you girl? You committed a sin with him, didn't you girl?"

Fargo felt each lash of the belt the girl received. His stomach knotted. His fists became useless lethal weapons. Someday he'd get his hands on Pa and that would be all for Pa.

The lashes and the screaming and the crying and the pleading to stop went on for what seemed like hours, even though it was in reality a relatively short time. And then it was done.

Poor Darcy cried into the spent silence.

Oh, yes, Fargo thought, *someday I'll get my hands*

*on that sonofabitch and it'll be all over for him. I'll
give him a taste of his own belt and then I'll stove in
the side of his head.*

Someday.

Someday, if I can ever get out of this crypt I'm in.

Deputy Andy Madden had a difficult time concen-
trating on the plump German girl he was trying out
on the second floor of Jody Tyler's whorehouse. All
he could think about was Tal Boatman and Boatman's
boast that he could lead Andy to Skye Fargo. Usually,
Andy tried to impress the gals with his "stay-ability"
as he liked to call it. But right now he didn't care. He
just got it over with. When the whore, who spoke little
English, looked up at Andy as he quickly dressed, he
read her expression with no trouble. "I no payee for
thisee," he said, in the same singsong way he ad-
dressed all foreigners, be that Chinee, Mexicanee, or
Germanee. "Missee Jodee take care of itee." The gal
looked baffled but he didn't give a damn. His prostate
felt better and he was in a hurry. He got out of there.

His horse was in back of the whorehouse. He oper-
ated under the delusion that this made his presence
at Jody's invisible. Who would expect that a deputy
sheriff, dipping his wick for free, could possibly be
clever enough to ground-tie his horse out back in
broad daylight? Because the house was on a corner
next to a vacant lot, nearly every man passing by
noted the color of the animal and said, "There's
Andy's horse. Someday his pecker's gonna fall off,
you just wait and see." The women passing by were
more refined in how they expressed themselves.
"Andy's poor wife. I don't know why she puts up
with it."

There was a good breeze from the south. Andy was
glad to be in the saddle. And alone. For a giddy minute or two, he felt like a boy again. No political prob-

lems to deal with—a lawman was a target for every political malcontent in town—and no marriage woes—a philanderer always had to cover his tracks with his wife and sometimes, the way Andy lived, that was impossible, and so he had to put up with a lot of yelling and screaming about how he was an unfaithful husband and a sorry example of manhood for his brood of kids.

But out on open range like this—

Pure pleasure until he came in sight of the Boatman place. Then the stomach started to go acid on him and the heart rate increased at least slightly and a vague headache began forming behind his right eye.

All he'd thought of since talking with Tal Boatman earlier was capturing Skye Fargo. Bringing him in dead or alive, he didn't much give a damn either way. He pictured himself riding down the center of town, trailing Fargo's horse behind him. Fargo slung over the saddle, of course. The voters would take one look at him—early thirties, virile, tough, handsome—and wonder why they put up with some old fart of a sheriff when a radiant god like Andy Madden could be elected into office?

There were a few things wrong with this little fantasy. Andy was actually forty-one, and he was virile only if he'd had enough sleep and wasn't hitting the bottle too hard, and was tough only when he brought out the brass knuckles or some such implement, and as for handsome . . . he couldn't remember any woman ever calling him that except his mother. And that had been when he was little. But . . .

. . . but—he would make a better sheriff than the sheriff the town had now. And that was for damned sure.

He didn't see Tal anywhere. If fact, he didn't see anybody. The Boatman place had the feel of being deserted. It gave him a momentary chill. He'd heard stories about how Indians would kill an entire family and then hide in a house, waiting for the next unsuspecting victim to come riding up.

He eased his rifle from its scabbard and then dropped down from his animal. He started to shout Tal's name and then thought the better of it. The suspicious silence made him too nervous to call out. He clutched his rifle.

He crept up to the window next to the front door and peeked inside. Nothing, nobody moving.

Sound, then: a jubilant jay, a lonely dog, a bored cow. Then wind all caught up in trees and bunch grass and long rough rows of wildflowers. Wind that sounded every bit as jubilant as the jay had.

And then another sound, one so pretty, so delicate that even Andy—who didn't claim to be sensitive or artistic in any way, who in fact disdained most higher forms of culture—got chills again. But these weren't chills of fear. These were chills of appreciation. He had never heard anything so beautiful—so achingly melancholy.

As if in a daze, he walked around the side of the place toward the three outbuildings in the back. The sound came from somewhere in the rear of the place. He had to find its source. Had to.

He vaguely remembered a story his older sister had read to him once, a "myth" she'd called it, about a young woman who sang with such sadness and beauty that all the young men fell in love with her. She was like a sea siren, drawing men to her with the simple grace of her voice.

The deputy knew who was singing, of course. It was just that nobody had ever told him what kind of lovely, elegant, captivating voice she had.

Andy Madden, tough-ass hombre (or so he imagined himself, anyway) walked around the red-painted shed and found himself in the presence of Maya Boatman, who sat on a tree stump, combing her long, radiant hair in the sunlight. And singing with a voice that threatened to undo him. And Andy Madden, tough-ass hombre, did not *want* to become undone by a voice and a song. How the hell would a fella explain something like that—*I swear to God, I didn't even want to touch her, I just wanted her to keep on singing*—to his pards in the saloon?

He cleared his throat.

She stopped singing as if she'd been shot dead through the heart. She prided herself on her hearing as many blind people did but she'd been so caught up in her singing that she hadn't heard him approach.

She turned around, facing him.

"That's some beautiful voice you got, Miss Maya."

"You startled me."

"Didn't mean to." His eyes assessed her body. A nice little tidbit, if you liked them on the thin side. "I was just looking for your brother."

"He left, Andy."

"Any idea where?"

She sighed. "I guess I may as well tell you. We had an argument and he just stormed off."

Now Andy Madden was many things, but foolish was not one of them. He sensed immediately what they'd argued about. Maya Boatman was a collector of lost and injured animals—so why not a lost and injured human animal like Skye Fargo? A desperate man facing the same gallows that he'd come here to help his friend avoid?

Sure, she'd help him. House him, feed him, heal him with those lovely hands of hers.

"Probably about that Fargo, huh?" he said.

"Why, yes, how did *you* know?"

"Oh, I'm just good at guessin' things, Miss."

She hesitated. Her sweet face wrinkled in displeasure. "That's why you're here, too, isn't it?"

"Miss?"

"You're looking for Skye, too, aren't you?"

He duly noted the use of Fargo's first name. He wondered if Fargo had put the pork to her. Now that would be somethin', wouldn't it? Hidin' him, feedin' him, healin' him—and then screwin' him on top of it. Yessir, if you had to be a man on the run, that was just the kind of good luck a fella'd want to have.

"He's a killer, Miss."

"He didn't kill Nan Miller, if that's what you mean."

Andy Madden smiled. "He didn't, huh? That what he tole ya, that he didn't?"

"That's exactly what he told me and I believe him."

"You know anything about his reputation in general, Miss?"

"If you mean have I heard of the Trailsman, yes. But that sort of thing gets exaggerated."

"You wouldn't say that if you'd seen the bodies of the men he's killed."

"I didn't say he was a saint, Andy. Traveling around the way he does, he's bound to get into scrapes. With his reputation, a lot of men are out to kill him. He doesn't have any choice but to defend himself."

Enough talk, Andy Madden decided then and there. This could go on the rest of the day. Yak got you nowhere.

"I need you to tell me where Fargo is."

His voice was different now. Harsh, raspy.

"Even if I knew, I wouldn't tell you."

"You ain't my sister, Maya."

"Meaning what?"

"Meaning there's only so much your brother can let himself do to you. But I can do whatever's necessary."

"If you hurt me, Andy, Tal will kill you."

Madden laughed. "Or die tryin', anyway."

In three steps he crossed to her and grabbed her shining dark hair. He twisted it so hard that she cried out and was forced to rise from the tree stump. He was a good foot taller than she was so it wasn't difficult to keep twisting her hair tighter, tighter.

"Where is Fargo, Maya?"

"I don't know." She could barely speak through the pain that turned her face into an image of terror and contempt.

"Maya, I really don't want to hurt you."

He grabbed the front of her dress and ripped it straight down to her hips, low enough that not only was one perfect breast exposed but so was the top of her pubic hair. It was the same lovely chestnut color as the hair on her head.

She screamed, her arms flailing about instinctively, trying to cover the exposed parts of her body.

He didn't slap her. He'd learned long ago that a sharp kick to the shinbone was a lot more effective and longer-lasting than a slap to the face.

The kick was so strong she collapsed in his grasp. The only thing that stopped her from falling to the ground was the hand he'd wrapped through her hair.

"Don't make me hurt you no more, Maya."

She cried now. Gently. The pain she felt was now joined with humiliation. Tearing the front of her dress had embarrassed her. She turned her grief and pain inward now so that the tears weren't about rage but about embarrassment.

"Tal won't have to kill you, Andy," she said softly between lips suddenly thinned out and hard. "I'll do it myself."

He smirked. "Oh, I forgot. He taught you how to shoot. And for a blind girl—"

"Don't underestimate me, Andy. You do any more to me, I'll kill you for sure."

The deputy thought a long moment. Her embarrassment was gone. Pure hatred possessed her now. He had to admit to a stray moment of fear. Funny, every once in a while you forgot about how women were supposed to be weak and obedient and not nearly as tough or vengeful as men—you had a moment when you saw that that theory didn't apply to all women.

As now.

"Well, I'll tell you what," he said, all fake joviality and would-be manliness. "Since you're gonna kill me anyway, I might just as well have my fun before I die, now, shouldn't I?"

He ripped the rest of her dress away so that in three simple gestures she stood nude before him in the sunlight, a lovely, white, gorgeously sexual creature that he was about to violate in such a way she would never forget.

"Well, now," he said, his voice clotted with desire. "Ain't you just somethin'?" He reached out and took rough hold of her left breast. It was even more exquisite than he'd imagined.

He laughed. "Even if you do kill me, Missy, it's gonna be worth it."

"You're the sheriff. You've got the key to the bank."

"You don't think I'd be the first person they'd suspect?"

"You don't have to worry about that."

"Yeah, and why not?"

"Because we'll make it look like somebody broke in instead of using the key."

"You got it all figured out, huh, Hap?" Sheriff Burrell said to his son as they sat on the front stoop of their house.

"Yeah, matter of fact, I do." He clapped his old man on the back. "You been wantin' to get rid of me for a long time, Pop. Now here's your chance. I'll wait for a seemly amount of time and then I'll just take off one day."

"With the money."

"Yep. With the money."

"And meanwhile, nobody'll be suspicious, I suppose?"

"Let 'em be suspicious. They can't prove anything."

"What happens if somebody sees us going in?"

Hap gave him one of those beaming smiles. "Two A.M., three A.M., who the hell's gonna see us, Pop?"

Sheriff Burrell had to admit that the notion of getting rid of his son sure sounded good. He knew by now that his son was never going to change. Too much arrogance, too much lust, too much greed. Every once in a while, a boy like that actually changed. He met the right gal or he got religion or he just plain and unaccountably grew up. But it wasn't going to happen to Hap, Burrell was pretty sure of that.

The trouble was exactly what he'd been saying: getting into the bank wouldn't be any trouble. Nor would figuring out the combination. Hap had long boasted that he was good with combination locks and Burrell had no doubt that was true. He knew that Hap had broken into a few places and stolen money from time to time. But this was different. No other business attracted attention like a bank. Anybody who happened to be out and about at that hour—anybody who happened to see a shadowy figure or two enter the rear door of the bank—why, that person would run right to the sheriff's office. And then the night deputy would round up a couple of men with shotguns and the three of them would post themselves at the front and back doors of the bank and insist that the men inside come out with their hands up. This was exactly the instructions Burrell had given his deputies over the years.

Then imagine the shock and anger when the deputy and his men saw Burrell and his son come strolling out.

Oh, Burrell was good enough on his feet that he'd have some kind of explanation for them. An explanation that might even make sense for the moment. An explanation that would calm the nerves of the night deputy to the point where he'd tell the men he'd enlisted to go on home, that this was all a misunderstanding.

But home in bed after the end of his shift, the night deputy would start to think about the excuse the sheriff had given him for being inside the bank in the middle of the night. And he'd begin to wonder. And then he just might stroll over to the bank that afternoon and have a little coffee with the bank president and say, *You know, the damnedest thing happened last night at the bank here.* And then they'd start talking. Now the bank president—a gruff old bastard named McGregor—he wouldn't have the automatic faith in Burrell that the night deputy did. And right away he'd be suspicious about the whole thing. The sheriff and that bullyboy son of his in the bank in the middle of the night? "That was pretty damned strange, wasn't it?" old McGregor would say. "The middle of the night?" And then the night deputy would finally be able to admit to himself—despite his loyalty to Burrell—that yes, the whole thing did seem pretty strange when you thought about it. And you didn't even have to think *hard* about it. *Middle of the night?* McGregor would say. *Middle of the night?*

"And then it all comes apart."

"What all comes apart?" Hap asked.

"The whole thing. Everything. It all comes apart." The dialogue between bank president and night deputy had been so real in Burrell's mind that he spoke as if Hap had heard it, too.

"So you're saying—what?"

"It's too risky."

"Riskier than somebody finding some bloody clothes that got that way the night a certain Nan Miller got herself killed in a hotel room?"

Every once in a while—and this was certainly one

104

of those times—Burrell would realize that Hap was of another species. He wasn't just "different," he wasn't just "spoiled," he wasn't just "selfish." He was a whole other species. There was just no other way to say it, to see it. He had the kind of ruthlessness you just didn't see in other human beings.

His own father. And it didn't mean a damned thing to Hap. His own father.

Hap said, "I'd just keep thinkin' about those bloody clothes, Pop. And I think you'll see your way to helpin' me out with that bank."

Fargo slept for a long time in the dank crypt of the root cellar. His entire body and mind were given into the arms of slumber. It was the sort of deep sleep he hadn't enjoyed in many nights. The sort of sleep that revitalized the body on a molecular level. The sort of sleep that brought strength and succor to flesh and bone alike. The sort of sleep that gave the mind back much of its focus and perception.

A good deal of his past fled through his dreams . . .

He remembered a copper-haired gal, a freckled feast of no more than 100 pounds of pure wild Irish beauty, a four-day weekend in St. Louis when they'd done everything possible a man and woman could do together.

He recalled especially a hot bath they'd taken together in an oversize tub . . . letting the steamy water intoxicate them with its soapy surface that was so much fun to slip a hand beneath . . .

He'd found her sex before she'd found his, slipping his broad fingers up inside her until she set her head back against the rim of the tub and closed her eyes and let him see just how crazy with need he could make her.

He'd made her crazy indeed, so much so that she soon enough slid her own hand under the water, finding his stiff, throbbing rod and began to tease the head of it with a knowing thumb. He was soon just as frenzied with animal longing as she was.

She eased herself up on him, half of her hidden under the soapy surface of the water, and slowly began to make him even harder with a slow side-to-side rhythm he'd never encountered before.

He could still feel her searing breath against his ear as she said, "Harder, Skye! Harder!" His upward thrusting making her throw her head back once again, and close her eyes. He wanted to make this the ultimate pleasure for her. He wanted her to forget everything but the orgasms that would soon come shaking and shuddering through her body to the point that it seemed she'd lost all muscle control.

It was an equally good romp for Skye, too. When he thought he could take no more, his upward thrust was so violent he bucked her clean up out of the water. She laughed and fell to biting his neck in a way that kept him hard enough to continue on until she was shouting and slamming her way to new heights of pleasure.

He awakened now and thought, remembered: *I am Skye Fargo*.

And with this simple thought most of his memories returned. Fargo—the lad. Fargo—the young man. Fargo—the wanderer. People, places, feelings—moments of glory, moments of humiliation, moments of peace, and moments of bloody rage and retribution. All the ticktock seconds that made up the life of the man some called the Trailsman.

The pleading letter from Serena. Talking to Curt. Starting to move around town, asking questions. Beginning to feel that he was making progress. And then the amnesia—

But now—

All the memories he needed—right up until the night he stood in front of the hotel room door. The door that opened on the bed. And the bed that hid the dead girl beneath.

He had the outline of that memory but none of the details—like a heavy black outline of a drawing that has yet to be filled in.

He walked into the room—

He found the dead girl—

And then—

So damned frustrating. It was as if he'd walked right up to the answer he needed—the identity of the person who'd knocked him out—only to have it snatched away by an unseen hand.

He had recollected every memory he possessed—or so that jumble of recollections had seemed—but the single identity that he most needed right now . . .

. . . nothing.

He had the sense that if he went back to that room that he could remember. He'd wait till night, till the circumstances were similar, and then he'd sneak into the room, look under the bed, and then—

—the memory he needed would come back to him. And the identity of the killer would be known. And both he and Curt would be free men again.

He stood up, cramped from sleep.

He'd had moments in his life when dark, finite circumstances like this cellar would have spooked him. Fortunately, this wasn't one of them.

I have to get out of here.

The need to flee had been strong enough without his memories. With them, he felt a kind of desperation. He had to get back to that hotel room. Had to fill in the missing blank in his memory. Had to confront the killer.

He walked over to the ladder. Climbed it making as little noise as possible. Heard the father and Darcy arguing.

"You do it, Darcy, or you're gonna get the switchin' of your life."

"We don't know he's the one."

"We sure do. Now you do what I say and right now."

"Won't you at least talk to him first, Pa? Get his side of things?"

"Don't need to *hear* his side of things, girl. Already know it. He'll say what all the devil's people say. He'll say he's innocent 'cause that's what the devil himself taught them to say. What's the point of wastin' time? And anyway, you know there's only one way to know if he's innocent or not."

"Maybe that's not true, Pa. Maybe that's not—"

The slap resounded like a whip lashing a tree.

"You take them filthy words back. I didn't make any of this up, Darcy. God give it to us in Scripture so we'd know who was a-lyin' and who wasn't. Now you take them words back, girl."

Fargo could barely hear the girl speak. "I take the words back, Pa."

"And you go do what I say."

"All right, Pa."

Darcy sounded defeated. The spirit she needed to talk back to her father was gone. She sounded as if she'd go along with just about anything now.

She wasn't gone long, wherever she went.

Fargo heard her coming in from outside.

"Now that's a God-fearing young lady," Pa said when she returned. "You start obeyin' me all the time like this and I can practically guarantee you that heaven's gates will open for you when the time comes. You understand me, girl?"

"Yes, Pa."

"You *want* to go to heaven, don't you, Darcy?"

"Yes, Pa."

"You say it like you're afraid to say it out loud. Speak up, girl."

"Yes, Pa. I want to go to heaven."

But there wasn't much conviction in her voice.

"I have to slap you again, Darcy?"

"No, sir."

"Then say it loud, and proud."

She shouted: "I WANT TO GO TO HEAVEN!"

"Now that's the way a God-fearing young girl *should* say it. Now give me that bag. How many you stick in there, anyway?"

"Three."

"Three? How come not six or eight?"

"I thought you were in a hurry."

"You're a-lyin' to me, girl." He sighed. "Give me that bag."

By now, Fargo had a pretty good idea of what was coming. The first thing he had to do was scramble back down the ladder and fast.

The trapdoor opened immediately. He could see the father outlined against the soft light of the day coming through the windows. And then he could see the bag open up and three rattlers come raining down alongside the ladder and landing on the earthen floor. They made soft, plopping sounds. Like pillows hitting the floors. But their angry hisses and rattles quickly took away such a benign image.

The trapdoor slammed shut.

Total darkness.

And Fargo left all alone with three rattlesnakes that probably weren't real friendly.

Probably not real friendly at all.

9

She was dead and he didn't know how it had happened.

She was dead and all he could do was stand there with his face in his hands, his trousers still down around his knees.

She was dead and he had absolutely no idea what to do.

A breeze dried some of the stinging sweat on his face, even through the splayed fingers through which he stared unbelieving at the unmoving form of the blind girl, Maya Boatman.

He hadn't even known it had happened right away. He'd been trying to force himself inside her. She had struggled throughout the entire ordeal. But this one time she'd bucked up underneath him with such fury that she'd moved them both something like half a foot. He'd wanted her too badly to stop. So he took his big paw of a hand and smashed it open-palmed into her face, not really trying to hurt her, just to stop her from stopping him from having his fun. And when her head had slammed backward—it had slammed into a small jagged boulder he hadn't noticed till then. It took him a moment to notice the blood, and that she'd stopped her struggling . . .

He tried to take her pulse but couldn't feel a damned *hint* of life.

That was when he stood up. All passion fled. He stood up and let the breeze dry him. He stood up and tried to make some sense out of this totally senseless death. He saw his life in shambles. He saw not only years in prison but shame and scandal for his family. And a rope just might be kinder than a prison term, however short. Because it was a Territorial prison, there were bound to be men inside he'd put there. And not always gently, either. Nights when he was drinking, he battered prisoners real good. And more than a few, he'd planted evidence on to make his case. So if some of those boys ever got together in prison to pay him back . . .

He pulled his pants up.

It felt kind of funny, standing over a dead girl with his trousers down and his sex hanging out there in the breeze. Disrespectful, somehow. He may have wanted to rape her, he reasoned, and he may even have been the unwitting instrument of her death, but he didn't want to disrespect her now. It didn't make any sense, his thinking, but that's how baffled and confused he was at the moment. Few of his current thoughts made any sense.

At the same time that Deputy Andy Madden was cinching his belt, Tal Boatman appeared on the edge of the woods. He'd taken the shortcut back home, a winding and shadowy trail through the thickest of the woods. He was pretty much lost in his thoughts and as a result didn't really see Madden at first.

Then he reined in his horse and sat his saddle pondering just why the hell Andy Madden would be out back of their place pulling his pants up and buckling his belt. There was both a latrine and an outhouse nearby but Andy wasn't anywhere near them. He'd stalked off after arguing with Maya because she wouldn't tell him where Fargo was. It sort of made sense that Andy Madden had stopped by here. See if ole Tal would tell him where Fargo could be found.

But it didn't make no sense that Andy Madden would be out back of the place pulling his trousers up.

"Hey!" Tal shouted.

Andy whipped around with such force, he like to have knocked himself over. His hand dropping to his gun, of course.

But the instant Tal saw Andy going for his gun, he went right to his saddle scabbard and pulled out his rifle.

"Why the hell you pulling down on me, Andy?" Tal said.

He saw Andy glance at something on the ground and wondered what it was. The bunch grass was so tall where Andy stood that Tal couldn't see the ground where he sat.

"You just scared me is all, Tal."

Sounded funny, Tal thought. *Sounded* very *funny. Like you do when you have a bad cold and you lose your voice sometimes.*

Being scared can do that to you, too, Tal thought.

He wondered why Andy kept glancing down at the ground.

Then Andy started walking toward him. Which was damned funny. Walking in such a way that it was obvious he didn't want Tal to see whatever he had been standing over.

"You all right, Andy?"

"Oh, yeah. I'm fine."

"You don't look fine."

"Comin' down with a little something, maybe."

"What was on the ground back there?"

"On the ground?"

"Yeah, Andy. On the ground. Isn't that what I asked you?"

"Nothin' on the ground."

He'd lulled Tal just enough that Tal was too slow bringing his rifle up when Andy fired at him. What saved his life—at least for the time being—was that

Andy got him in the shoulder instead of the heart. And that Tal pitched off the horse as soon as he got shot, hitting the deep grass and making himself hard to find from Andy's perspective.

Tal didn't mean to lie here and be killed. He sighted his rifle and fired. But the shoulder wound had made him shaky and fuzzy. He had more firepower than Andy at the moment, that was true. But the blood leaking from his shoulder was making him too unsteady to fire off a decent shot.

"All I want to do is take you in," Andy said.

"You're lying, Andy. For some reason you want to kill me."

"Just take you in is all, Tal."

"Bullshit. What's goin' on here? What're you hidin'?"

And when it came to him, the powerful strength that only rage can give you filled his body and soul. "Where's my sister?"

Andy paused just enough—and looked just miserable enough—so that Tal knew that something had happened to Maya. Something that Andy had done to her.

Tal's aim was better than Andy's, as his shot grazed Andy on the left side of his head.

He was going to kill the lawman sure thing, now. He didn't give a damn about Skye Fargo or anything else. He'd treated the girl so bad sometimes—hell, look how he'd argued with her just a few hours ago—so bad sometimes that he couldn't face his own guilt now. All he could do, all he wanted to do, was kill Andy Madden.

Snakes.
Darkness.
A great combination.
Skye Fargo had two lucifers left and he couldn't afford to waste them.

He stood in the corner with a small chunk of rock he remembered from the last time he'd used a lucifer. Thrown accurately, and with enough force, it could smash in the head of a rattlesnake, no doubt about it. The force wouldn't be any trouble. Fear of snakebite filled with enough anger to ensure that he would bring plenty of force to the task.

And that left two problems, one being the accuracy of his throw. And the other being the number of snakes. Three. Even if he got lucky once—or even twice—that left a third time he'd need to be lucky. And nobody had luck like that.

People had the impression that rattlesnakes were noisy. They were but only when they were about to strike. The rest of the time they were as silent as any other serpent, slithering quietly across dirt, sand, rock—whatever their environment happened to be at the moment. So silent, so stealthy that they could slither up to a leg, shimmy the length of a mattress, or even glide along a stretch of coarse grass without being detected in any way, if they chose to. The Trailsman had been around enough rattlers in his wandering years to know that they weren't especially interested in killing people. They did it only when they felt threatened or only when they needed the sustenance of heat.

They were somewhere in the darkness of the root cellar. Fargo didn't have a clue where. But he was spooked by them. Three of them. They could well be collected in a far corner, not interested in him at all. Or they could be a couple of feet away, sensing his body heat, making what they thought was an innocent approach.

Snakes.

Darkness.

Fargo scratched himself. Now wasn't that a damned dumb reaction to have? But dumb though it might be, he had the sense that something was crawling all over him. Maybe not snakes but some other kind of creepy, crawly *thing* that was both silent and invisible but was on him nonetheless.

Dank, dark root cellars tended to produce eerie fantasies. Especially when three rattlers had been turned loose in that same dank darkness.

He needed a gun. What he needed most of all, he corrected himself, was luck.

Footsteps on the floor above. The trapdoor opening. Good ole Pa. "You enjoyin' yourself? Them rattlers maybe won't get ya right away. But you mark my words, they'll get ya sooner or later."

"But, Pa—"

"You hush now, girl. This is between me and Fargo here. Maybe you don't care that he killed your sister, but I do."

"I didn't kill her. The only time I ever saw her, she was dead."

"The devil's tongue. Lies. That's all the devil tells and that's all you tell, too." He tittered, sounding daft. "You enjoy yourself down there."

Fargo took the few moments of dying daylight to search the cellar for any sign of the snakes. He didn't see any. Which meant they were in the back near him somewhere, in the densest part of the gloom.

"You want the real killer and so do I," Fargo said. "You turn me loose and I'll find him for you in twenty-four hours."

"I can hear the fear in your voice, Fargo. I bet my poor daughter sounded like that before you killed her. She probably begged you, too. That's the part I can't stand. Hearin' her beg you. Ever' time I try and sleep, that's all I can hear. The way she must've begged you. You probably enjoyed yourself, didn't you, Fargo? Pretty young girl like that beggin' you for her life. Probably made you feel like a big man. Important man. And actually killin' her probably made you feel even better, didn't it? Well, you'll be beggin' me before this is over, Fargo. And you know what? I'm a-gonna show you jest the same kind of mercy you showed her. And that's none. Yessir, that's none."

The trapdoor started to close. Fargo shouted, "Even if you kill me, you can't be sure positive that I'm the one who killed your daughter. In the back of your mind, you'll always wonder if you got the right man. You'll go into town and just about every man you'll see—you'll wonder maybe it was him and not Fargo at all. Or him. Or him. And then you won't hear your daughter beggin' for her life anymore. You'll just hear your own mind questioning you. Did Fargo really do it? Is the real killer that man walking right towards me? Or the man I just passed? Or the man who I see every Sunday at church? It could be any of them. And that'll drive you crazy."

The trapdoor slammed shut.

The girl said something in protest but her exact words were muffled.

Fargo was still tensed up from all the angry words he'd delivered unto the madman known as Pa. He moved, in the newly refurbished gloom, a few steps to his right, placing himself next to the straight-backed chair.

He had no idea that upon the seat of the chair sat one of the rattlesnakes. He had no idea that by merely brushing past the chair he'd set off a complex series of alarms within the snake's nervous system. For the rattler, everything that happened in the next few moments was reflex. Nothing personal against the human giant whose close proximity terrified the reptile. Nothing personal at all. The human giant was just being . . . human. And the rattlesnake was just being . . . rattlesnake.

The snake struck with such speed that Fargo didn't have a chance of moving away in time. The rattling sound and the strike itself were essentially simultaneous. Now Fargo's own *human* central nervous system duplicated the mechanics of what the snake's had done. Warned him. Sent alarm signals so desperate and singular that Fargo's entire body and mind had but one mission—to escape the attack.

But the snake's fangs sank deep and true, its poison exploding into Fargo's bloodstream. By this time— only two, three seconds after the attack—Fargo was able to pitch his body away from the chair and the snake. Not until he was moving swiftly through the darkness did a terrible thought come to him. He didn't know where the other two rattlers were. What if he spun away from this one only to fall prey to a second or even a third?

He landed with his back against the cold, hard-packed wall of earth. Only now did he have a moment to realize the impact of what had just happened. The realization came in the form of severe, radiating pain in his thigh. The snakebite. The *poisonous* snakebite.

Panic.

That was his next thought. Panic was now as much a potential enemy as the snakes were a real one. He had to find some simple way to extract the poison from his system.

The other thing he had to do was clear his mind of all the snake stories he'd heard. How death from reptile poison was a particularly nasty way to die. The fever and delirium, the choking, and finally the suffocation.

Pa would be happy. Good old crazy Pa.

Pa would be very happy.

Andy Madden still got the next shot in.

True, Tal should've had the advantage. After all, Tal held a gun on him. But what Andy did was throw himself to the ground, making himself invisible for a very important moment or two. In that time, when

Tal was shouting for him to show himself, Madden was able to stand on his knees and start shooting at Tal. Clean, quick shots.

. Tal took the first bullet in disbelief.

How the hell did I lose control of this situation so quickly? he wondered.

The second bullet got him in the stomach.

It was a funny thing. A bullet in the stomach should've dropped him right there and right now but somehow he managed in his rage to push ahead. He wanted to see what Madden had been keeping from him. Tal had a pretty good idea what it was. His sister's body. The human mind was a strange thing. He'd treated her so bad most of his life but now that she was in danger—or might even be dead—all he could think of was getting close to her. Nothing else mattered, as Madden discovered. He kept right on firing, Tal kept right on coming, seeming not to feel the bullets that tore away chunks of his flesh and penetrated through bone and flesh alike into some of his vital organs.

When he saw her lying there, naked and bloody, Tal let out an animal cry of wrath and doom that gave Andy Madden chills. Never heard any human make a noise like that. Tal had always been spooky. But this was spooky even for Tal.

Tal dropped to his knees next to his sister, taking the tatters of her dress and tenderly draping them over her naked body. Her poor little slim body. She shouldn't be lying out here naked this way. It was an offense against heaven.

Tal didn't hear Madden crawling through the long grass. Soft evening breeze. Madden smelled the texture of heavy dust on the grass as it slapped against his face. Hadn't smelled grass like this since he was a little boy. Which was a funny thing to think of when you were sneaking up on a man and about to kill him.

Madden knew he could finish Tal off now. He was

already thinking about how he'd handle this, both of them dead. Simple enough. He came upon Tal kneeling next to his dead sister. He'd obviously just finished ravishing her. Madden had been so outraged that he drew down on Tal and ordered him to stand up. But Tal had his own plans and they obviously didn't include getting arrested. He opened fire on Madden. And Madden returned the favor.

The bullet that took Tal's life entered his body through his forehead. Bull's-eye. Death was damned near instant. There wasn't any flailing or wailing, either. He just dropped down dead and that was that.

Dropped down dead but not before he was able to squeeze off a single lucky shot that took Madden in the left eye. You take a shot in the eye and there's no time there, either, for any flailing or wailing. You are just plain dead.

They killed each other. That wasn't unknown in the old west, a shoot-out that ended with both men dead. And it happened again here today.

A cool wind came up, soughing the thick, tall grass. Both men were laid out on their backs. Not long from now various animals would appear to do what came naturally. Another eight, nine hours, the men's faces would be pretty much gone completely.

Off by herself, Maya Boatman lay beneath the tatters of her dress.

The animals would try her on for size, too.

By sundown, Sheriff Henry Burrell had reluctantly accepted the idea that he was going to help his son rob the bank. He even knew who he was going to blame for it.

When Hap came back from the creek, where he'd bathed in the bone-numbing water before he climbed into clean clothes for another night's carousing, Burrell said bitterly, "It isn't just robbing the bank, Hap."

Hap was combing his hair. He was as vain as a

woman. "I guess I don't know what you're talking about, Pop. But then I guess I don't know what you're talking about most of the time, anyway." His smile was a sneer. He picked up his old man's glass of whiskey and threw back a drink. Then he slammed the glass back on to the table. Always pushing, he was. Seeing just how much the old man could or would take before exploding. He'd been like this all his life.

"What I mean is that I'll have to blame somebody else for the robbery."

"All the derelicts in this town, it shouldn't be hard."

"We're talking about somebody's life here."

Hap, buttoning his shirt, said, "Don't go all teary-eyed on me, Pop. Just pick somebody and pin it on him."

"It'll have to be one of my deputies."

"Make it Madden."

"Can't. Madden knows too much about me. He'd tell everybody everything the minute I brought his name up."

"Then make it Sullivan."

"Sullivan? You forgetting that little girl of his? The one with the palsy? He goes to prison, what's his wife and daughter supposed to live on?"

Hap paused to look at his old man. "I'm sure you don't want to hear this, Pop. But I really don't give a damn what his wife and daughter have to live on. It's my own ass I'm worried about. I want out of this town—good damn riddance and I promise you you'll never see me again—that's what I'm worried about. And anyway—" Here he was pushing the old man again, saying something that he knew would really grate on the old man's nerves. "Anyway, that daughter of his is about the ugliest little girl I ever saw."

Burrell grabbed his glass so hard, he damned near smashed it just with his big hand. But he wouldn't rise to the bait. He wouldn't give Hap another droning sermon on decency. Burrell wasn't a decent man himself, that was for sure. But he didn't have the kid's meanness. "That leaves Manning."

"He doesn't have an ugly little daughter, huh?"

"Save that tough-guy talk for your friends. I'm trying to make a decision here."

"Well, Manning sure isn't very bright."

"He also drinks a lot. I could sneak into his room over at the hotel and slip the key into a pocket. We could find it there in the morning and accuse him of taking the extra bank key from my desk and robbing the bank. We could say he hid the money somewhere. He wouldn't hang just for bank robbery. I'd do what I could to make sure he got the lightest sentence possible." He was talking to himself. Hap, shining his boots with a rag, wasn't listening. He'd leave the details to his old man. That's what fathers were for, anyway. Details. "He doesn't have a wife. I don't think he has any kin except maybe back in Ohio."

"Well, there you have it, Pop. The whole thing nice and neat. You put it all on Manning and while you're doing that, I'm riding away with a whole lot of money. Never more to return."

He went to the peg where his holster rig hung. He strapped on his gun like a professional. Which he wasn't. He was slow and he was inaccurate. But he didn't have to worry about his lack of prowess. He was smart enough to keep his bullying inside the town limits. Nobody was going to shoot him here, not with his old man wearing that silver star.

"So when do you want to do this, Pop?"

"Sooner the better."

A smirk. "You want to get rid of me, huh?"

"Damned right I do."

"And here I thought you'd get all teary-eyed when I finally left this hick burg."

"I like it here."

"I know you do. And that's one more reason I don't have any respect for you. Speaking man to man, I mean. You settled for some stinking little town like this. And now you're too old to do anything else with your life. I'm not going to get trapped that way."

"No?" Burrell snapped. "Then just how *are* you going to get trapped, smart boy?"

Hap put his finger to his chin and stared off, as if he were in deep thought. "You know how I see myself at age thirty? I'm some kind of kingpin in some Frisco casino or something. I've got these real fancy clothes on and I'm walking around this room filled with important men and important women. Every one of them knows who I am. And every one of them is afraid of me. I'm ruthless and they know it. So ruthless they'd never think of trying anything against me. I even sleep with their wives and they know there's not a damned thing they can do about it. Their wives want me too much and if the menfolk tried anything on me, I'd destroy them."

He looked down suddenly at his poor, pathetic old man and said, "Now, if that's a trap, Pop, leave me to it."

He walked to the door, turned around. "Tomorrow night you're going to make me a rich man, Pop, and I sure do appreciate it."

Fargo needed to get the poison out of his thigh and he was damned if he knew how he was going to do it. He felt his way around in the darkness. He knew how Maya Boatman had to live her life, the poor young woman. But with her it was perpetual darkness.

He made a lot of noise stumbling into things. If there was a snake close to hand, the damned thing would be alarmed for sure by Fargo's blind clumsiness. A few times, he even stumbled, tripping over holes in the dirt floor, landing on one knee and forcing himself back up again. A snake caught you on one knee, off-balance that way, you were doomed for sure.

He had to stop to take a leak. There was a slight burning sensation in the urination. He had no idea what that meant. The poison in his system was starting to spook him. Every single bodily function from breathing to a faint itchiness on his wrist seemed suspicious and somehow tied to the snakebite. Or was the fear itself starting to make him a little bit crazy? He'd seen that happen innumerable times to men around him. The mind played tricks on you; in the right circumstances, your own mind could help do you in as fast as an arrow through the heart or a rock crushed against your skull.

He searched.

Most of the time he was half-afraid to reach out and touch anything. What if he accidentally touched a rattlesnake? Two poisonous bites would kill him for sure. Hard enough dealing with the bite he had now.

But what choice did he have?

Pain from the bite, a pounding headache that might or might not have something to do with the bite, and the first dry-mouthed inkling of dehydration—these were his companions as he searched the cellar.

Voices. Not arguing this time. Just—voices. The father and the daughter. Once again the specific words were lost on him. He kept right on searching. Interesting as the voices might be. They told him nothing.

But when the door slammed upstairs, he stopped, curious about what was going on. No shouting, no sense of the father being angry. Silence after the slam of the door. Prairie silence. Rich, deep, peaceful. He imagined—in a kind of fever-dream—what it would be like to stand on a hill and look up at the rolling stars and the gleaming moon. There were times when he felt the stars spoke to him in a way he didn't understand, as if, as some Indian tribes believed, the stars could summon warriors from the planet Earth. Enjoyable as this daydreaming was, he shook his head to clear it. He had to focus on the here and now. Day-dreaming would only sap his draining energy. Day-dreaming would only help delirium overwhelm him.

He waited a few moments longer and then resumed his search. His useless search. He wasn't going to find anything and he knew it. But he had to keep looking. His only hope.

The cold sweat came without warning. He shivered beneath its icy lacquer, slumping against the wall despite his fear that a snake might be lurking on or near it. Indentations had been dug low along the wall at several points. Perfect for snakes.

He felt the first signs of being faint, of succumbing to the darkness that lapped at his consciousness every few minutes now. He wondered how much time had passed since the rattler had bitten him. He was beginning to lose both his sense of time and place.

He stumbled against the wall again. Shivering. Dry-mouthed. Confused. But no. He had to fight against this process of declining power. He was his only hope. He forced himself from the wall, forced himself to stand straight and tall.

In this burst of determination, he realized that his only hope lay upstairs. In the world of human beings. There was nothing for him down here except maybe another snakebite. Somehow he had to climb that ladder and somehow he had to open that damned trapdoor. At the moment, he had no idea how he was going to do this. He would just have to improvise when he reached the top of the ladder.

He walked, wobbly, across the span of the cellar to the ladder. He had to grope and hunt as he went, fearing he might bump into something that held a rattlesnake. But the serpents were apparently at rest.

He felt an idiotic glee when his hand touched the ladder. Whoa there, boy. He was getting way ahead of himself. Just because his hands gripped either side of the ladder didn't mean he was on his way to freedom. Didn't mean that at all. He put one boot on the lowest rung. And then the cold sweat came again and again without warning. He was simply covered with an oily coldness that sapped both his strength and his perception of things. For instance, the trapdoor suddenly appeared to be much farther away than it had been before. The ladder itself had become something from a nightmare, its rungs seeming to multiply and multiply until it seemed to stretch to the heavens. How could he ever climb anything that steep?

All he could do was fight against the hallucination he was having. One part of his mind accepted it as real but fortunately another part knew it was not. He was in a root cellar. This was a common ladder with an eminently climbable number of rungs. A trapdoor awaited him at the top. A simple, common trapdoor that he would or wouldn't be able to open. He had to banish the hallucination. He had to keep his mind focused on reality.

He had to climb.

He climbed six steps and then fell off the ladder, landing hard, his head smashing against the earthen floor with such force that he fell into unconsciousness once again.

A confusing miasma of memory, nightmare, semi-awareness of pain, and freezing cold . . .

Sounds he could not recognize. Then: light he could not recognize—a square of muzzy light from above.

Dreaming of his boyhood . . . a fishing hole . . . a warm afternoon . . . a feeling of comfort and well-being that he would rarely know again after the rite of passage that made him the man he was. . . .

. . . A skeletal hand reaching out for him beneath a bed . . . summoning him in whispers to an erotic encounter . . . a hideous grinning skull that had once been a lovely young woman's face . . . calling his name with such soft lust that he felt both revulsion and desire at the same time . . . she was dead, wasn't she?

A skeleton picked apart by time and the elements? But she continued to whisper his name and he had to fight the inclination to slide beneath the bed with her.

Phasing in and out of reality.

At last a sound that was familiar—the sound of heavy material being ripped. His sense was that his trouser leg was being ripped free. . . .

Somebody asking him questions. Him . . . giving answers. Or some part of him. Automatic answers.

He felt himself form the word "snakebite."

The chill was upon him now with such fury that the castanetlike sound he heard was that of his teeth clattering together.

A fierce wound, even fiercer than the snakebite itself. A blade cutting deep into his flesh. The touch of human lips upon the bite. Him trying to sit up . . . to see what was going on . . . to see who had come to help him.

The chills replaced by searing heat. Fever. The transition from one to the other must have taken at least a little time but in his condition, time was nothing he could calculate. Everything . . . past and present . . . was merging.

He returned to the shadowy hotel room. The corpse beneath the bed. Turning to see somebody about to bring down the handle of a gun. To knock all memory from him. And once again, he saw the person doing this. Saw but could not put a name or even sex to this silhouette. Cried out against this person. But it was too late, of course.

He had to identify that person. Had to . . .

On the ladder again. Waking or dreaming, he couldn't be sure. Then he got a splinter in his hand from the wooden rung above him.

He was awake. You didn't usually get anything as specific and real and painful as a splinter in your hand in a dream. Not unless the splinter played an important role. But this was just a minor splinter inducing minor pain . . . no special significance to the crazy narrative of the dream.

He really *was* climbing a ladder.

Somebody pressing a small hand to the small of his back, coming up the ladder behind him . . . trying to keep him from tumbling off again. Hurting himself even more.

A period of . . . overwhelming fever. He felt so hot that his skin should be blistered by now. Felt so hot that when something—a rag—was put coolly to his forehead, his entire body spasmed in response. He thought of opium addicts he'd seen and how their entire bodies shook when they needed their drugs. Surely, he looked like that now. Surely, he felt like that now.

Delirium . . . a part of his mind recognized that he was delirious. He tried for a time to fight against it but then simply gave into it. What choice did he have?

Being taken somewhere. Familiar, if distant, smells of his big Ovaro stallion. Being taken somewhere. But where? And by whom?

Dreams, nightmares, memories . . . and through the mist of all these images . . . he realized that his hands were roped to the saddle horn so he couldn't fall off of the horse.

A phantasmagoria of sounds and scents . . . night. A coyote somewhere. The smell of creek water. Splash of beaver on creek's edge. Aroma of drying horse dung.

Where was he going? Who was taking him there? And why? The fever, which had still not broken, sheathed him in what felt like flame. Somehow, sometime in his delirium, somebody was pouring water from a canteen into his mouth. The cool water felt good against his seared flesh.

Darkness . . .

A bed. A . . . kitten licking his face. A girl's voice shooing the kitten away. Water being poured into him.

Sleep. Deep, deep sleep.

The skeletal hand reaching out for him in nightmare again . . . the seductive voice calling for him to join her.

The kitten . . . the persistent kitten. Coarse tongue on fevered flesh. Whiskers tickling him. The girl's voice again. "Bad kitty. Bad kitty. Now you leave them alone."

Drifting.

Them? he thought after a time, recognizing the significance of what the girl had said. *Who was "them?"*

Trying to sleep. Trying to block out all stimuli. Wanting to find again that soft deathlike center of unconsciousness where there was total rest, total peace. Where he was aware of nothing, nothing at all.

"You think he's going to be all right?" someone asked, an older female voice this time.

"I hope so," said the girl's voice. "I don't know what else I can do."

"You've done so much already," the young woman said. "For both of us."

"Well, you're giving me a place to hide out. That makes us even."

"That's nothing. A little food, a place to sleep—"

"If my father figures out where I am, you won't be happy you're hiding me. He'll tear this place apart."

The young woman sounded on the verge of tears. "This seems to be a night for tearing things apart."

Little bitch.

Darcy had been in such a hurry to flee that she hadn't even bothered to close the trapdoor. It stood wide open, as if she was proud of what she'd done. Tom Miller smacked his fist into the wall of his cabin.

There had been a brief church ceremony he'd wanted to attend. Darcy, the little bitch, had vomited and said she was too sick to go. *Lord spare us the deceptions of unholy children.*

As he stood there inside his cabin, night fully in

128

bloom now, rich-smelling as a flower bed through the open front door, he tried not to imagine his daughter's body defiled by Skye Fargo. He knew that was what this was all about. The handsome face of the killer had aroused his young daughter's satanic and lustful impulses. She would give herself to him. She would nurse him back to health—she was very good at taking care of ailing people—and then their bodies would conjoin in the vilest of sins.

He had to find her. Somehow stop the inevitable from happening.

And then he heard them. Their rattle. In the root cellar.

He'd best collect them before he departed.

He found the burlap sack Darcy had used to bring them inside from the pit outdoors. He took the sack and descended the ladder.

He didn't need a lantern. He had what hill folks called the Sight. He was one with the snakes and could see them even in the dark. His parents had taught him that the godly had no truer friend than the serpent. The serpent could tell the truth about a person faster than any man ever could. As a small child in the deep South, Tom Miller had been bitten many times by rattlesnakes. Once and only once had he taken ill. His parents had understood that this was a way God had of testing them. If they had true faith, God would heal the boy. If their faith was not true and deep, they would try to heal him themselves. They waited two days. The boy went into convulsions. The boy's skin blistered. The boy went mad. But, curiously, he did not die. God chose to heal him. And though he had endured many rattlesnake bites over the years, none so much as gave him a low-grade fever. His faith protected him.

So he took no precautions now that he was down here in the root cellar. No precautions at all. He sensed each one of them in the gloom. Then he would snatch them up one at a time and drop them into his burlap sack. The one that had bitten Fargo, he was especially careful with. This one, he knew, had been blessed by the Lord to do very special work here on earth.

Finished, he climbed the ladder, took the writhing burlap bag outdoors, and put the serpents back into their pit, to be called upon again when it was necessary. Whenever God whispered in his ear.

Then he went in search of his lustful and prideful daughter and the man known as Fargo. He would kill them both.

10

"I don't know how he's still alive," Maya Boatman said. "After all he's been through."

"He's starting to come back a little, though."

"My grandfather had an expression, 'You couldn't kill him with a pickax and a six-shooter.' I think Fargo must be like that."

"They're going to hang his friend this afternoon, aren't they?"

"Unless he can figure out some way to stop them. And in his condition—"

Fargo made a sound. Exactly what the sound was, neither the woman nor the girl knew. Was it a sound he made consciously? Was it simply the muttering of dream sleep?

They both stood by the bed where he lay. Maya reached down and touched his forehead. "His fever's broke."

She tried hard not to think of her dead brother. Much as she'd disliked—even hated—him at times, he'd tried to come to her rescue. Both he and the deputy had thought she was dead. Not only did Andy prove himself to be a bastard at the end, but he wasn't worth a damn when it came to taking a person's pulse. When her brother came back and got into the fight with the deputy, she was struggling back to consciousness and witnessed the whole thing.

Now, she felt pretty good. Better than Fargo, apparently.

For his part, Fargo also had his struggles. The time of Curt Cates's hanging stayed in his mind. He knew his friend to be innocent. He couldn't let him die.

He began the long swim up through the murky fathoms of injury, poison, lost memory, and pain. That was the noise he'd made a few moments ago—the noise of bone-weariness meeting the noise of determination. Curt had once saved his life. No way could he do any less for Curt now.

He got his eyes opened and said, "Where am I?"

Maya Boatman leaned into his eyesight. "In good hands, Skye."

"How'd I get out of that cellar?"

Another familiar face leaned into his frame of reference. "I helped you, Skye," Darcy said.

"I'm most appreciative to you two ladies."

Young Darcy obviously liked being called a "lady."

"Now I've got to get up and get going."

"You can't do that, Skye," Maya said.

"Sure I can. And I'm going to."

"But why?" Darcy said. "Burrell'll kill you. If my father doesn't first. They're all looking for you, Skye. They—hate you."

"I owe Curt Cates my life. I can't run out on him now. Besides, I need to talk to that undertaker."

"Stan Thayer?" Maya said. "What for?"

"He's the only one I haven't talked to, not looking to kill me, that had a look at both bodies."

"You're not really thinking of going into town, are you?" Darcy asked.

"I don't have any choice. That's where Thayer is."

"But Darcy's right. They'll shoot you on sight."

Fargo didn't listen to them. Couldn't afford to. He had to convince himself he was strong enough and wily enough to do what he needed to do. So he blocked out the negative opinions, and somehow man-

aged to steel himself enough to sit up without screaming. Headache pounded, snakebite had left him chilly
and weak. But he needed to sit up so dammit he sat
up.

"You're in no condition to go anywhere," Maya
said.

She was probably right, Fargo thought. But that
didn't mean he wasn't going to keep right on going.
"I'd appreciate some food and a little whiskey if I
could get it."

"Skye, you're not going to—"

"Please," he said. "We're almost out of time. Now
I need some food."

Beef and a boiled potato was served to him at a
small table five minutes later. He ate like a starving
animal. He didn't worry about table manners at this
point.

Fargo startled the two females by surging up from
the table where he'd picked his plate clean. Before
either woman or girl could get a hand on him, Fargo
had found his holster, his Colt, and his boots, and was
getting himself ready to lurch out the door and take
care of business.

First Maya implored him not to go. Then Darcy
took over. All the time they did their imploring, Fargo
was checking his Colt, his gun belt, his sight. He kept
splashing his face with cold water from a jug. They
could see him trembling—the aftermath of the long
and searing fever—but he knew he needed to feel
even chillier if he was to come truly awake.

By this time, they'd given up trying to talk him out
of it. All they could do was pray silently that the Lord
would be with him and that he'd succeed in what he
was trying to do. Unlikely as that was.

Sheriff Burrell had used the bank key on only one
other occasion.

A drunk had reported seeing a moving light inside

the bank just after midnight. The night deputy knew that a bank key was kept somewhere in the sheriff's office but he wasn't sure where. He risked waking Burrell up. Burrell was gracious. He saw how nervous the deputy was. Burrell went to the office and got the key. Then he went in the back door of the bank while the deputy and the drunk stood watch outside. The bank was empty. The drunk had been imagining the light. Burrell could have gotten mad but he didn't. The bank was the single most important business in town. Most businesses kept their money there. If the bank ever got cleaned out—

That was the thing, Burrell thought, opening the special false-bottomed drawer in his desk. He'd come down early to the office. They'd hit the bank later this evening. He wanted to make sure the key was still there—even more, he wanted to make sure that he'd thought this through sufficiently.

On the one hand, this would give him the opportunity he'd been wanting to cut Hap free. It was a terrible thing to think about your own flesh and blood, but Hap was bad in every way you could measure a person. And even if he came back after spending all the money, it would at least give Burrell a year or two's peace of mind.

The key was there.

He took a deep breath, sighed it out.

This thing could go wrong so many ways. He tried to force these thoughts from his mind but it wasn't easy. So many ways it could go wrong. . . .

"Quiet night."

Burrell looked up at the new kid deputy, the assistant to the night deputy. Now why couldn't he have a son like this kid? Perry was his name. Tim Perry. He was everything Hap wasn't—hard-working, polite, wanting to make his mark in life. He was only nineteen but he was a substitute usher at the Methodist church and he played the accordion at barn dances. If he drank, it wasn't much and it wasn't often. Even the prisoners liked him, which was pretty funny when you thought about it. Were prisoners *supposed* to like deputies?

"Yep, it is a quiet night, Tim."

"You seem sort of quiet tonight, too, Sheriff, you don't mind me sayin' so."

That was another thing about Tim Perry. He made a point of reading your moods. Of knowing just how to approach you, just how to handle you when you were having a bad day or a bad night. Hap didn't give a damn what your mood was. If he wanted something, he tormented you till he got it, and the hell with whatever mood you happened to be in.

"Oh, just thinking about the past, I guess."

"Yeah, I do that a lot, too."

Burrell smiled. "You do? You haven't got that much past to look back on."

"Sure, I do. I had a good time growing up. Hard work; my pa lost his arm, remember, when I was seven, so I had to kind of pick up the slack around the farm. But there was plenty of time for fishin' and huntin' and things like that. I've got a lot of good memories."

Burrell literally ached to hear such words tumble from Hap's mouth. A little gratitude for the things Burrell had always given him; a little sentimentality about growing up in Burrell's house; a little fondness for the time he'd spent under Burrell's roof. But no, there'd never be any of that with Hap.

"Where's Coburn tonight?"

Tim Perry tapped his nose. "Bad head cold. You should hear him. Sounds like a foghorn. He's pretty sick. But that's no problem. I'll take his half of the businesses, too."

The night deputies divided up their duties, chief among which was checking to see that all the doors were locked on the town's various businesses. People who had a gripe against the sheriff's office always said that the lazy bums didn't do much of anything except walk around and rattle a few doorknobs. Well, what they didn't seem to realize was that that was among the most important duties a lawman could have. Preserving the well-being of a town's businesses. Because businesses moved on. No business wanted to stay in a place where the law wasn't any use. You see a man whose store has been robbed three or four times, you see a very unhappy citizen, one who just might consider leaving town and setting up somewhere else.

So, dammit, every single night, twice a night in fact, the night deputy and his assistant walked their rounds. And if there was even the slightest hint of trouble, they took care of it.

"He's sick an awful lot lately, Tim."

They both knew what kind of "sick" he was. Bottle sick. Though neither of them wanted to say it because Coburn had a wandering wife he didn't know how to deal with any way short of alcohol. The trouble was, Burrell had carried him about as long as he could afford to. Pity could extend only so far. Then you had to start worrying about how the man's performance was affecting his job. It sure wasn't doing Coburn or the sheriff's office any good, the way Coburn was always "sick" these days.

"I'm sure he'll be fine real soon," Tim said confidently.

That was another thing Burrell liked about the kid. Loyalty. He'd had plenty of opportunity to run the night deputy down—maybe even to hint that he wanted his job. But he didn't. Never said a bad word about Coburn. Quite the contrary. Always stuck up for him whenever Burrell said that maybe he needed to "talk" to Coburn.

Tim nodded and said, "Well, I'd better go make those rounds."

Sometimes, Stan Thayer liked to have a little fun with them, the corpses. He'd put on too much makeup and make them look spooky, or he'd put a dress on a man, or he'd make a woman look like a saloon gal. The truth was, after about corpse one thousand, the work got pretty routine. Even the smells did, too. Oh, the dead still smelled, especially the newly dead, but it was the same old smells over and over.

Stan was at work in his basement when he heard the sound on the stairs. Who'd be coming here at this hour? And who'd be rude enough to just let himself in without knocking? He smiled. The one thing he didn't have to worry about in his calling was getting robbed. *You want a spleen? A glass eye? A bag of feces?* He could just see the surprised face of the robber when such a bounty was offered.

Then who the hell is on the stairs? he thought as he saw the lantern on the edge of the table flicker.

Just as he was turning away from the table where he had a dead woman laid out so he could begin the process of putting her into her dress, he saw a dead man on the steps. The dead man was packing a Colt that was aimed right at Stan Thayer.

The dead man's name was Skye Fargo. He was paler than the corpse Stan Thayer was working on at present. His eyes were just about as lifeless, too. The last time Stan Thayer had seen Fargo, the Trailsman had been a vital, imposing figure. No more. He moved slowly, as if he might suddenly drop. And the way his gun hand trembled, it was easy to see he didn't have much strength in him.

He came into the room and looked around.

I'll be in a room like this someday, Fargo thought. *Some ghoul like Thayer'll be working me up to make me look all new and shiny for the mourners. The ghoul'll stuff me into a coffin so everybody can say*

*how nice I look, and then somebody'll announce that
there's some food and whiskey in the other room. And
the whole thing'll turn into a party.*

If there was bitterness in his thoughts, it was quickly
banished by the realization that he'd done the same
thing himself. Tied one on at a good many funerals,
forgetting all about the poor bastard in the coffin. It
was probably only natural. You paid your respects and
then you went on with life. That was about all you
could do, Fargo thought, till it was your own time to
have a ghoul start working you over.

"Looks like you brought me some business,"
Thayer smiled. "Just climb in that coffin over there
and I'll fix you right up."

"You know who killed those two girls."

"I do?"

"Yes. And you're going to tell me who it is."

"Now how would I know something like that, Mr.
Fargo? You're not only weak, you're delirious."

Fargo spat on the floor. "Somebody got to you.
How much did you get to keep your secret?"

"You're a very cynical man, Mr. Fargo. I'm a simple
undertaker. Nobody would pay me for anything except
burying them and even then all their kin do is bitch
about my charges."

"How much they pay you?"

The ghoul was about to smile again but Fargo
moved with such sudden and violent force that the
sneer died stillborn on the undertaker's lips.

Fargo slashed the gun down across the man's face,
knocking him back into the table where the dead
woman lay. The dead woman went flying off the table
and crashed onto the floor.

Fargo was moving close to the ghoul again when a
voice from the stairs said, "Drop your gun, Mr. Fargo,
or I'll save the sheriff some trouble and kill you
right here."

The woman was short, stout, gray-haired. The way

138

she squinted, you could tell she didn't see all that well in this dim lantern light. You could see the long-buried girl trapped like a ghost in all that flesh and hard muscle. She'd probably been pretty once. But no more. In her flannel nightgown, she looked tough enough and mean enough to beat the hell out of Fargo and Thayer together.

"You don't even think of hurtin' my son any more," she said. "Now drop that gun of yours."

"He needs to tell me the truth," Fargo said.

"And you need to drop your gun before I start puttin' holes in you."

He had only one chance and he took it. He flung his Colt directly at the lantern on the edge of Thayer's worktable. The lantern smashed against the floor, chasing everything into heavy shadow.

Mrs. Thayer fired off two shots that were loud as thunder. They were just close enough that they sent Fargo to the floor.

He crawled around the table as she started her search for him. He crouched on the far side of the table.

"Where did he go?" the woman bellowed.

"I'm tryin' to put this damned fire out!" Thayer snapped. Apparently the lantern had started two boxes ablaze. From his angle behind the table, Fargo could see Thayer's boot kicking the boxes hard.

Fargo waited till the woman took four more steps, in the meantime groping the floor for his Colt, which he retrieved and jammed into his holster. With her fourth step, which brought her less than a foot away, he flung himself up to her.

The rifle boomed again, a startled shot fired at the ceiling.

The law—or what was left of it—would be coming for sure. Midnight gunfire at the mortuary was bound to attract attention.

He wrestled the rifle away from her, threw it across

the room, and took off running. He had an idea. He just hoped it worked. If it didn't, he wasn't sure what he'd do. Maybe there wouldn't *be* anything left to do.

Twenty minutes later, Stan Thayer did what Fargo hoped he would do. He came out the back door of the mortuary, went to the barn where he kept two horses and his funeral vehicles, saddled a mare, and headed out.

Fargo had no idea where he was going but that was all right. He figured it would be someplace interesting.

The moon had an ancient, sinister look to it tonight, the way it must've looked when Aztecs sacrificed their virgins to it. He'd heard a lecture on Aztecs once. They worshipped the moon, offering up thousands and thousands of human sacrifices to it over the span of their reign.

But it wasn't Aztecs that made Fargo uneasy now. Maybe it was the hooting and crying of all the night creatures in the darkness. Maybe it was because Fargo was starting to freeze his balls off. It was cold enough that he could see his breath. The drop in temperature woke him up just fine, but between the arrogant look of the moon and the cold, he felt as if he was traveling across the surface of an alien world.

At one point, Thayer stopped suddenly, sat his saddle for a moment and then suddenly turned around. Was he aware of Fargo behind him? He must've been aware of something or somebody. He wouldn't do this unless he was suspicious, would he?

But then Thayer seemed to satisfy himself that it had been only his imagination. Nobody was following him. Who would follow him at this time of night? Fargo? No, his mother had run him off and scared him off. He had to laugh about that one. People didn't fear Thayer but they sure feared his mother. Hell, *he* feared her. You get her riled up the way Fargo had tonight and—

They reached a hill and—

And once again, Thayer turned around. This time, he seemed to have a sense of somebody on his trail for sure.

But then he urged his mare onward, over the hill, and down into the hollow where Curt Cates had his place.

But why the hell would Thayer go to Curt's place? Fargo didn't know that the two men were enemies, but he didn't know they were friends, either. And even if they were friends, why would Thayer be stopping by in the middle of the night? The farmhouse was dark.

Fargo dropped off his stallion, ground-tied it, and then hurried to the crest of the hill where he hid behind a wide oak tree. Below, everything was cast into shadowy silvered relief.

Thayer tied his horse to a slim birch tree and walked up to the door. He walked without any hesitancy. A lot of self-confidence for a man here on such a late-night mission.

The knock was short, loud, somehow threatening even though it was lost to the steady wind that soughed the autumn trees.

He had to knock twice more before a lantern was turned up inside. Then there was another wait before the door was opened.

Serena Cates stood in her nightgown, holding her lantern high. The wind took their words. But Fargo didn't need to hear what they were saying. Thayer's actions said it all.

He slapped Serena across the face with a force that drove the young woman back into the house. He followed her inside, slammed the door. Even above the wind, Fargo could hear Serena's cry. He had the sense that Thayer had slapped her again.

Fargo began his descent down the long, sloping hill. He remembered Thayer stopping twice to check his back trail. Was Thayer at one of the windows now, waiting to open fire as soon as he glimpsed Fargo?

Fargo extracted his Colt from its holster. He moved deep shadow to deep shadow, hoping this gave him sufficient cover. He half expected shots to come from the house at any moment.

Thayer's horse whinnied as it scented Fargo. Fargo hunkered down behind a stack of wood.

Thayer appeared in the window. He glanced around. He had his gun in his hand. He stood there for some time, looking around.

Fargo was still wondering what the hell he was doing here in the first place. Strange enough that he'd call on Serena in the first place . . . but to call on her so late . . .

Thayer moved away from the window.

A scream. A tearing sound. Another scream. A slap so violent it sounded like a gunshot.

He didn't wait, couldn't.

He stood up and began to close the distance between himself and the farmhouse. He kept his Colt ready to fire. But it didn't sound as if Thayer had much interest in him at the moment. It sounded, instead, as if Thayer had rape on his mind.

He crept to a side window and had his suspicion confirmed. But it wasn't a rape. At least not now.

Serena was on her knees, servicing Thayer. The undertaker had ripped away the top of her nightgown so that her bountiful breasts were exposed from the light of the lantern perched on a nearby table. As she knelt there, her eyes were fixed on Thayer's face. The gun he held angled close to the side of her head.

Fargo just hoped that Curt never had to find out about this . . .

Fargo eased himself around the house to the front door. There was only one thing to do now and that was to rush the place. Kick in the door and find out for sure what was going on here. Why would Serena have anything to do with a ghoul like Thayer?

But he hesitated. What if Thayer decided to kill Serena the moment he heard the door kicked in? Could Fargo kill him fast enough to save Serena? He doubted it.

Fargo wasn't much for waiting. Patience was not high on the list of his virtues. Much as he wanted to charge inside, he didn't want to get Serena killed, no matter how much she was betraying Curt.

He pressed his ear to the door. Thayer was making animal noises. Things were ending up. Fargo gave it a minute or so longer. Just when Thayer was enjoying his climax was the perfect time to—

11

Just before two A.M., Hap Burrell said, "You ready?"

"Hap, maybe we should think this over."

And then the old man said it. Just said it straight out, said it out loud there in the shadowy depths of the alley that ran along the side of the stuccoed bank building. "You killed two women, Hap. Maybe you shouldn't get the money, too."

"*I* killed two women? What're you talking about? *You* killed those two women."

"The hell I did," Burrell said.

"Then how'd you get blood all over your clothes?"

"I saw you hurrying out the back door of the hotel. You were movin' so fast, I figured somethin' must be wrong. When I got up there, she was dead. I slipped in all the blood and got it on my clothes. You were in her room."

"I was in her room all right looking for a good time. But she was dead when I got there."

"Hap—this ain't no time to bullshit me. You really didn't kill her? Or the other girl?"

Hap grinned. "Hell no. I'm a lot of things, but not a murderer. So if you thought I killed them gals, what was you so afraid of when I found them bloody clothes? It's pretty funny when you think about it."

"I figured you knew I wouldn't turn you in, and

144

figured another scandal involving my son would cost me the next election. So if we didn't kill her, who the hell did?"

"Right now, I don't *care* who did." Hap nodded to the ebony shape—a deeper black than the shadows—of the bank's back door. "All I care about is gettin' my hands on that money and gettin' out of town."

"They'll figure out who did it, Hap. You'll be long gone and I'll be left here to face the consequences."

"You can always skedaddle, too."

"With you, you mean?"

Hap smirked. "Sure, old man. You'd make a great traveling companion. You've got arthritis, gout, and you fart all night in your sleep. I don't see how Ma put up with it all those years. You're a pig, old man. And I sure as hell don't want you as a traveling companion."

It was funny, Burrell thought. Everybody considered him to be so tough. But nobody was tough when it came to dealing with an insolent child of your own. A kid of your own could hurt you in a way nobody else could. Maybe this was because you saw not just your kid standing there smirking—but your own failures standing there, too. Most kids don't turn out this selfish and crazy without help. And Burrell had helped him on his way by never being around. By letting his beloved wife pamper and spoil Hap to the point where the kid believed that he could do anything he wanted and get away with it. There'd always be Mama—and Pop if necessary—to extricate him from any problem.

"I'm not goin' in, Hap," Burrell said. "And neither are you."

Moonlight glinted off the cold weapon Burrell held straight out from his ribs. The gun was pointed right at Hap's heart.

"You won't shoot me."

"It's over, Hap. All that's left is for you to ride out

of here. I'll be doing the same in a couple of days. I need to wrap up some business first. We've got a new deputy to help out."

"Your little pet Tim Perry."

"He's a good young man."

The way he said it seemed to bother Hap. "Bet that's not anything you ever said about me."

"Just ride out, Hap. Now. Before anything happens."

"Yeah, Tim Perry'll be making his rounds about now. Maybe he'll arrest me."

Burrell was surprised that Hap was so jealous of Tim. Maybe it was that obvious, that Burrell wished for a son who'd turned out the way Tim had.

For a moment, he felt sorry for Hap. This was one of the few times he'd ever felt that the boy had feelings other than greed or rage. He could be hurt and now—Burrell suspected—hurt deeply. He felt sorry for the boy and sorry for himself. They'd lived their lives at such cross-purposes. They'd never shared anything except bickering and threats.

"Like I say, Hap. Please get out of this town—out of this alley and away from this bank—before something bad happens. You can ride out clean and start your life again somewhere else. That's a big gift, Hap. A very big gift. Now please do what I say."

"I want the money, old man. It'll take me half an hour to get it and then I'll be gone. That's all I'm asking."

"I'm sorry, Hap, I just can't—"

In the old days, nobody ever would've pulled this off. Not on Henry Burrell they wouldn't have. Henry standing there with his gun aimed right at Hap's chest. And Hap ducking under the gun and running right at the old man. Henry was still fast enough to turn away from his lunging son, but too slow to avoid Hap's hard, strong fingers on his wrist. Hap snapped the wrist bone in half, forcing the weapon to fall from the old man's grip.

Hap grabbed the gun. "You could've just handed it over to me, old man. Saved us both the trouble. Now I want the key to the back door of the bank."

Pain lanced up from the broken wrist, like steel claws dragging across Burrell's forearm. "I won't give it to you, Hap. Just please ride out. Please." He had never felt older or more helpless. The pain from his wrist was so sharp and relentless—Hap looked like an angry stranger—and Tim Perry would be along any time now on his rounds. Bad things were going to happen. Bad things that terrified the old man.

Fargo moved.

He hit the door so hard with his shoulder, the pine frame around the door broke off as the door itself was flung inward.

Serena was just getting to her feet.

Thayer was just buttoning up his trousers. He didn't have time to complete a full turn to see who'd come smashing through the door. Fargo jammed his Colt away. He didn't need it. He lavished a dozen punches on Thayer with such fury that the undertaker dropped his gun to the floor of his own volition. Fargo slammed his fists into Thayer's face, throat, chest, and then worked his way back up to Thayer's face again. Once more he found himself in a frenzy of rage. He had to work off his feelings of helplessness. Even with his memory restored, even with his physical strength coming back, he hadn't been able to help Curt or to find the killer. And Thayer paid the price for this failure.

Thayer's face was streaked with rivulets of blood. His left eye was closed from Fargo's relentless fists. As he tried to stagger free of Fargo's anger, Serena said, "That's enough, Skye."

He barely heard her. And he certainly didn't obey her.

The shot she fired missed his head by no more than an inch. He was still so lost in his violence that he didn't respond. But when the second bullet scorched past him, he took sudden note. And stopped.

A trick of the light—the simple return of his entire memory—Fargo would never know why that at this exact moment he recognized the person who'd knocked him out in the hotel room the other night.

But at just this angle—in just this light—he saw and recognized his hotel room assailant. It had been Serena.

She must have seen this recognition in his face because she said, "I knew you'd figure it out someday, Skye."

"You killed those two women." He wasn't asking a question. He was stating a fact.

"I didn't have any choice, Skye. They were taking him away from me. That Potter bitch wasn't just satisfied with Curt, she took Paul, too."

And then, in that same light, at that same angle, he noticed something else for the first time. The faint suggestion of madness in her gaze and voice, a subtle element of suspicion and fear that could well lead her to. . . .

"He wasn't unfaithful, Serena."

She scoffed. "I'd expect you to stick up for him. You owe him your life."

"He wasn't unfaithful. He really wasn't."

"That's what my first husband said, too."

Fargo remembered the troubled and evasive way Curt always talked about Serena's first marriage. The husband getting drunk and drowning. . . .

"Did you kill your first husband, Serena?"

"You wouldn't blame me, Skye. Not if you'd known him. Not if you'd known how he'd cheated on me. . . ."

Thayer, lying on his back across the room, began to moan. Fargo doubted he was seriously hurt. He was probably in a lot of pain. But he'd recover soon enough.

Then he turned back to Serena. As much as he wanted to hate her, he couldn't. Yes, she'd been willing to let Curt hang. Yes, she'd killed two people. Yes, she was probably on the verge of killing him. But she wasn't an adult—she was a tortured and angry little girl who couldn't separate her fears from reality. Simply having the thought that Curt had been unfaithful made it so. At least to her.

"I would have told you if you hadn't gotten so violent," a frail-sounding Thayer said from the corner. "She's the only woman in town who has a pair of those Alberts. I could see their tracks in the blood at the hotel room. I knew right away she killed that little gal." Alberts were dressy, pointed-toe, side-button shoes that were all the fashion back East.

He slumped back down, moaning again.

That explained why Serena had complied with Thayer's sexual desires. He'd been blackmailing her.

And then he saw her as she was that night in the hotel room—she was the one who'd knocked him out, temporarily causing his memory to fade.

"Serena, let me help you."

"No, Skye. He deserves to hang, so let him hang."

"But he didn't do anything, Serena. He didn't cheat on you. He didn't."

She raised the gun. A weariness had come into her face. He knew she was going to kill him. She'd probably kill Thayer, too.

"I'm sorry about this, Skye. I really did like you."

"Serena, please listen—"

"But you're just like all men. You cheat and lie and—"

One shot. One shot that seemed louder than a thousand shots. One shot that caught her right in the heart. One shot that had been aimed at her shoulder, a shot that would merely wound and not kill. But at the last moment, seeming to anticipate the sudden appearance of Fargo's gun from his holster—at the last moment,

Serena had leaned forward. And Fargo had already fired. And the bullet—

She was absolutely quiet when the bullet ripped into her. Blood bloomed across her chest. As she fell forward, her head smashed against the edge of the table. And when she hit the floor face first and hard, she grabbed on to a chair. As if she wanted to pull herself up again. But her thin white hand slipped away. She died without making a sound.

Thayer was struggling to his feet.

"You were blackmailing a crazy woman, Thayer. That make you proud of yourself?"

He'd been thinking maybe he'd been a little too rough on Thayer. But since he'd figured out the blackmail angle—

He gave Thayer a strong swift kick in the stomach. Thayer had just started puking when Fargo walked out of the farmhouse door.

Tim Perry made his rounds half an hour later. Henry and Hap Burrell had decided to hide in the alley behind the bank, wait until Perry appeared to try the back door then go on with his other rounds.

While they waited, Henry Burrell began to feel even older and wearier than he had when he'd been arguing with Hap. He'd hardly been an exemplary lawman, taking the same route most lawmen did if they'd confess to it. The rich people of a town hired you and they expected you to do their bidding. For the most part.

There were two unwritten laws for the average sheriff. You would cover up about anything if a rich person—or a rich person's son or daughter—was involved. But you wouldn't cover up a murder.

And you wouldn't cover up anything serious involving your own family. They could raise a little hell, they could get in fights, they might even knock up a girl. But if it was anything that involved serious theft or violence—then you had to treat them like anybody else. If you didn't, you had to move on to some other town.

He supposed, as he waited here in the darkness, that he should feel relieved. Soon enough, it would be all over. Hap would have his money and be gone. Henry would take his meager pension and retire to someplace Hap could never find him. He had no illusions about Hap and tonight's robbery money. Hap would go through it quickly and then come looking for the old man for a "loan." It was a terrible thought to have but he never wanted to see his son again.

"He's gone," Hap whispered.

"Yeah."

"So we can go in."

"Yeah."

Hap gave him that cold smile. "You should be happy, Pop. You're finally getting rid of me."

Henry watched as Tim Perry turned right at the mouth of the alley. So much of life was luck of the draw. You were born to a certain person, a certain place, a certain time—those things that people didn't think about much played such a part in your destiny. Now if a man was lucky enough to have a son like Tim Perry . . .

"Let's go, Pop."

Holding back was pointless now. They were going to do it. Hap would get his money and ride far away. And Henry would ease on out of town over the next few weeks.

Henry slipped his arthritic left hand into the pocket of his trousers and felt the cold metal of the bank key. "May as well get it done."

"How's it feel to be on the other side, Pop?" Hap grinned.

"I been on the other side a long time, Hap," Henry said. "It was the only way I could keep you out of prison."

Hap laughed. "You're feelin' sorry for yourself again, old man. Ma always said that, remember? That you felt so sorry for yourself? I don't think she thought that was real manly. She never said anything direct to me—but that was the sense I had of it. You always feelin' so sorry for yourself, I mean."

Just when you thought he couldn't hurt you any more, he did. Hap was always quoting his mother where Henry was concerned, quoting these words and feelings she'd never expressed to Henry because they were derogatory, hurtful. The thing was, Henry could never tell which things were true and which things Hap made up on the spot just to hurt him. It was clear that she'd confided in him—it was clear that she'd expressed misgivings about her husband—it was clear that she and Hap had had more than a few laughs about him. There were different ways of being unfaithful. You could cheat with another person, and you could also ridicule your mate behind his or her back. That's how his wife had cheated him. By being more intimate with Hap than she'd ever been with Henry.

There wasn't much to it.

They walked the short, dusty distance to the back door of the bank. Henry took the key and inserted it. The lock gave way and Henry pushed the door inward. The only light was the dim dull half light from the streetlamp outside. The banker had insisted that one of the lamps be positioned directly in front of the bank for just such a moment as this—when robbers were about.

Being inside the closed bank evoked different reactions in the two men. Hap was exhilarated. This was the dream of every tinhorn criminal in the entire West—being inside a bank late at night. Henry felt as if he'd committed a terrible sin—an intrusion into a domain that would cost him his soul.

Hap had insisted that he had the tools necessary to

152

open the vault. Henry didn't want to know about them. He stood guard at the window while Hap went to work on the safe.

The first few minutes went well. Henry was able to contain his nervousness. Keep his eye steady on the street. Do his job as lookout man.

And that was when the crash came, a sound so loud in the quiet night that the dead in the graveyard were probably opening their eyes.

What the hell had Hap done, anyway?

12

Tim Perry was on his way back to the sheriff's office when he heard the noise from the bank, which he'd just passed a minute ago. In the silence, the sound was as loud as an explosion.

Perry was startled, of course. That was his first reaction. His second reaction was to be curious. His third reaction was to be scared.

With a wife at home who was having a difficult time with her first pregnancy—there'd been two miscarriages before—her fear for him had started to take its toll. The other day she'd told him that every night he went to work, she had to fight off dreams of him being hurt or even killed in some violent encounter. Even though he'd explained to her how quiet the town had become in the past few years, even though he'd explained that no local lawman had been killed in many long years, even though he explained that he never got into any situation he didn't think he could handle—despite all his reassurances, she still teared up when he left and clung to him like a child when he returned.

He was scared.

Was this the moment Karla had been dreading, warning him about? Some incident in the middle of the night, nobody much around, him alone against a gunny or a pair of gunnies?

But the badge meant something to him. People figured he was being self-important and corny when he said that. But it was true. A lawman had saved his father from a beating by two drunken saddletramps one rainy Saturday afternoon. Little Tim had been with him, pounding his fists uselessly into the saddletramps. Then a U.S. marshal appeared and arrested the two men at gunpoint. Tim had never forgotten how grateful he'd felt to that lawman. His father could easily have died that day but for the appearance of the marshal. He saw the difference that the lawman had made in his young life. He wanted to make the same kind of difference in the lives of other folks. So call him self-important, call him corny, call him anything you want. The badge and the job and the responsibility meant something to him.

He hitched up his gun belt, drew his weapon, muttered something resembling a prayer, and headed for the alley running flush with the bank.

Hap still couldn't believe it. All he'd done was back into a three-drawer card file and the damned thing had fallen over backward. Even a full two minutes after the crash, he still couldn't hear anything except the echoes of the crash. He stood gaping down at it like some dumb animal encountering something it had never seen before—something incomprehensible.

Hap had never sweated so much before in his life. Even the bottoms of his feet were slippery with sweat.

He looked at the safe ahead of him. Had to get to work. Fast. Especially now with all the noise.

He just hoped that Tim Perry hadn't been anywhere in the vicinity to hear the crash.

"What the hell happened?"

Hap looked up out of his daze.

His old man stood there.

"Why the hell'd you come in here?" Hap snapped.

"Why the hell you think? What happened?" Then

Burrell's eyes followed the angle of Hap's gaze to the floor and the card file. "How'd it happen?"

"Who cares how it happened, old man? Now you get your ass out there and stand guard. Let me worry about things in here."

"Doesn't look like you're doing too good a job," Burrell said.

Hap pointed to the door and made a face, the way he would with a naughty child. Except this was his father.

Shaking his head, Henry Burrell turned and left the shadowy interior of the bank.

Tim Perry stood at the head of the alley, half wishing he'd brought along the rifle from the office. The rifle, now there was a weapon.

Nobody was in the alley.

That was the good news *and* the bad news.

Good because maybe it meant that whoever had been in the bank had run off. Bad because it could also mean that they were hiding in the bank, getting their money and waiting for somebody to respond to the crash.

Somebody just like Tim Perry.

Hell of a job he had ahead of him, Fargo thought, as his stallion moved quickly through the night toward town.

Curt Cates would be happy to hear that he had been cleared of the murder charges. He would be devastated to hear that his wife had done the killing. And was now dead.

The first thing he'd do when he reached town was wake up Henry Burrell and lay the whole situation out for him. Everything he told Burrell could and would be backed up by the undertaker Stan Thayer. Fargo would make a deal with the slippery mortuary man. Fargo wouldn't tell anybody how Thayer had blackmailed Serena into having sex with him. And in turn Thayer would be Fargo's witness. He wanted to punish Thayer in some way but sometimes the world didn't work that way. Sometimes justice meant cutting a deal. And this was one of those cases.

He spurred his stallion toward town.

It was sort of funny in a sad way.

Here came Tim Perry tiptoeing down the alley toward the rear of the bank. And here out the back door, stepping into the alley itself, came Sheriff Henry Burrell.

The two men stood looking at each other, clearly outlined in the moonlight. Each man held a weapon. Each man felt his pulse increase three-fold. Each man was horrified at the sight of the other.

Perry didn't want to believe what he was seeing. His first thought was that Henry had been up at this hour for some very good reason and was near the bank and had heard the crash and had come here to check it out for himself.

But when he saw the sick and anxious look on Henry's face, he knew that Henry had had some connection to the commotion inside the bank.

Henry tried to make a good show of it. "All under control, Tim. Dog managed to work the back door open and was chasin' all around in there. Knocked over a card file."

"Dog, huh?" He kept moving toward Henry. He kept his gun at stomach level. Henry's gun was drawn, too.

"Yeah," Henry said. "Dog."

"Mind if I go inside and look around?"

Henry obviously forced himself to stay calm. "I got her all locked up again."

"Dog broke through the lock, huh?"

Henry shrugged. "Guess somebody forgot to lock it after bank hours."

"I see."

They stood still, staring at each other. Somewhere an owl cried out its displeasure with the night.

"You're out awful late, Henry."

"Couldn't sleep."

Tim tried to figure out a way to ask it. Then he decided that the simplest way was the best way. "What's goin' on in there, Henry? And no more bullshit about a dog, all right?"

"Nothin's goin' on, Tim. Except just what I said."

"Henry, I want you to put your gun down."

"Well, I'll be damned. Have you been drinkin' tonight, Tim? I'm the sheriff, remember?"

"You're not the sheriff when you're breakin' the law."

"Breakin' the law? What the hell're you talkin' about? I heard a noise and went into the bank to see what was goin' on."

"And it was a dog, right, Henry?"

"You damned right it was a dog, Tim."

But the sick face was back on Henry. Tim felt sorry for him. Whatever was going on here was something bad. Tim had the sense that Henry didn't want to be a part of it, either.

"Henry, I want you to put your gun down."

"What happens if I don't, Tim? You gonna shoot me?"

"Unless you shoot *me* first."

Henry was about to say something but suddenly there was no time to say anything at all. Hap came charging out from the rear of the bank, a suitcase in one hand and a gun in the other. Before either his father or Tim Perry could say or do anything except freeze a moment in surprise, Hap shot Tim three times in the chest. He wasn't aiming especially, just firing. He was a good enough shot that the bullets hit in reasonable proximity to the heart. Tim fired twice above Hap's head—fired as he was collapsing to the ground.

"What the hell you doin', Hap?" Henry screamed. He realized at that moment that his voice had never sounded like this before. Some kind of terrible aggrieved sound that he'd heard previously only in the throats of wild animals when bullets ripped into them.

"What the hell you think I'm doin'? I'm gettin' out of here!" He nodded to the suitcase. "I cleaned it out, Pop. Every paper bill they had."

But Henry wasn't listening. He'd turned around and was now walking over to the fallen body of his deputy Tim Perry.

"You know, Pop, if I didn't know better, I'd say you cared a lot more about Tim there than you ever did about me."

Then Hap gave him one of those cold Hap smiles.

Fargo reached the town limits at the exact moment Hap Burrell opened fire on Tim Perry. This late at night, it wasn't hard to follow the echoes of the gunshots.

By the time he dropped off his stallion, jerked his Colt from its holster, and approached the alley in a crouch, Henry Burrell was kneeling down next to his deputy, looking frantically for any sign of life.

"Need you to ride out of town with me, Pop. I may need a hostage."

Henry looked up. Even though he was several feet away, peering from behind the edge of the front of the bank, Fargo could see the tears gleam in Henry's eyes. "I'm done with you, Hap. I wouldn't lift a hand to help you no matter what you said. You want to ride out of here, you ride out alone."

Fargo ducked back before Hap could see him.

"Get up, Pop."

Henry stood up. "You going to kill me, Hap? That's

where this has been leading all your life, hasn't it? To kill me, I mean. Your own father." Henry gently lifted his gun from its holster, tossed it in the dust. "I'm makin' it easy for you, Hap. I won't even defend myself." He glanced back over his shoulder. "But you better hurry, Hap. Hear those feet? All that shootin' woke people up. They're on their way here now. If you're gonna shoot me, you better make it quick."

"They won't shoot me if you're with me, Pop. Now I said stand up."

Fargo could almost feel Henry Burrell's weariness as he said, "Maybe you'd be doing me a favor anyway, Hap. Maybe it's my time."

Hap said, "You sonofabitch."

He moved to where his father stood hunched over Tim Perry. His father was just now putting pennies on Perry's eyelids.

Hap kicked Henry so hard in the back that Henry fell into the dust next to Perry. He didn't stop there. He kicked him again, this time near the base of the spine. "I told you to get up, old man, and I mean now."

Fargo made his move. "Back away and toss your gun to the ground, Hap."

To Hap, Fargo wasn't much more than a silhouette. But enough moonlight glistened on the barrel of Fargo's Colt to make him a damned dangerous silhouette.

"Well, well, Mr. Fargo. You're a lot better than I thought you were. Had half this town looking for you and they still couldn't find you."

"Back away, Hap. And toss your gun down."

Hap kicked the old man so hard in the side that Henry rose a good inch off the dusty alleyway. Henry made a moaning sound and then seemed to collapse not only physically but spiritually as well. Almost as if he was dead. Fargo could see the tears streaming down Henry's face. It didn't take much to figure out what he was crying about. Even if he survived this night, the life he'd had was over now. He'd run out of hope that his son would ever be anything more than a spoiled thug. And now he was a killer as well.

Hap must have figured that Fargo had been lulled into some kind of momentary disinterest because he did a very stupid thing.

He spun to the right and was about to pitch himself to the ground where he could get a clear shot at Fargo. He moved quick and he moved well, too. But nobody could move that quick or that well in front of Fargo's gun.

Hap had time to fire just once before four of Fargo's bullets opened up streaming holes of blood in Hap's chest. Hap hit the ground the way he'd been wanting to. The trouble was, hitting the ground wasn't doing him any good at this point. Hap was already dead.

Moments later, the townspeople arrived. Most of them were bundled up against the autumnal chill. Most still rubbed sleep from their eyes, yawned, and fired up cigarettes, pipes, and stogies to help them come fully awake.

Two of the women helped Henry to his feet. He was truly an old man now, bent over, weeping openly and without shame.

An hour later, dawn blooming, Fargo and Curt Cates sat at a table in the only café open in town. Curt had heard it all now. Unlike Henry Burrell, Cates took his bad news dry-eyed and quiet. "This hasn't hit me yet, about Serena."

"The big thing is you aren't going to hang."

Cates drank coffee and stared out the window. "I've got to get out of this town."

"Probably a good idea."

"It's gonna be bad when it hits me, Skye. About Serena, I mean. Right now I'm so tired and confused and—"

"Get some sleep, put your place up for sale, take your best offer, and head for the train depot."

"That sounds pretty good, Skye." They both watched as Sheriff Henry Burrell walked out of his office and stood on the boardwalk, looking around. "I never thought I'd say it, but I actually feel bad for old Henry. I guess we've both had to face the same thing. The people we loved let us down pretty bad."

This was the part Skye Fargo wasn't much good at. Curt Cates was going to get maudlin. As it looked like Maya and Darcy would take care of each other, this was a good time to leave.

He stood up and shook Cates's hand. "You'll start a whole new life for yourself, Curt. And all this'll fade in time."

"I sure hope so, Skye. Thanks again for everything."

Skye Fargo wasn't sure where he was going when he climbed aboard his Ovaro stallion. All he knew was that he wanted out of this little hellhole of a town. And fast.

True to his name, three minutes later with his memory restored, he did just that.

Looking Forward!

**The following is the opening
section of the next novel in the exciting
Trailsman series from Signet:**

**THE TRAILSMAN #271
St. Louis Sinners**

*St. Louis, 1860—
The sins of the father may be visited upon the
son, but the child who walks alone is
threatened with damnation at every turn—
where salvation's last hope lies on the cold
end of a smoking gun.*

It was bright outside. Fargo walked out the swinging
doors of Dustin's Red Dog saloon, only to find a
fifteen-year-old kid hanging onto the Ovaro's reins
and tugging with all his might.

Now, Fargo knew damn well that the Ovaro
wouldn't go off with anybody but him—and Fargo also
had a few beers in him, which in this case heightened
his sense of humor—so he just leaned up against the
building and watched for a second.

The kid pulled and pulled, trying to get the black and white paint stallion to take even one step, but he might as well have been trying to haul off Pike's Peak with a lasso made of thread. The Ovaro just stood there stubbornly at the rail, and snorted calmly, whiffling his nostrils.

The kid tugged and pulled and swore, then hauled on the reins some more, but no dice.

Finally, Fargo couldn't keep his mouth shut any longer. He said, "Having some trouble, son?"

The boy, tallish, dark haired, and owning the promise of growing up into a quite handsome fellow—if he didn't get hanged for horse theft first—said, "It's this damn horse, Mister. Can't get the son of a bitch to budge!" To the Ovaro, the boy said, "C'mon, Charlie, old boy! Get a move on!"

The kid was a good liar. Fargo would give him that. Why, if he didn't know different, he would've believed that the Ovaro belonged to the kid.

Fargo said, "Well, why don't you hop up on him? Ride him out. Maybe he just doesn't want to be led."

And then, biting his cheek, he waited for the festivities to begin.

"That's an idea, Mister," the oblivious boy said gratefully. "Don't know why I didn't just do that in the first damn place."

Settling his too big hat on his head, the kid slung the Ovaro's reins around the horse's neck, took hold of a handful of mane, and slid his foot into the stirrup. He was almost in the saddle when the Ovaro put his head down and bucked out his hind quarters big, but just once, throwing the boy flying.

In fact, the kid landed on his ass in the middle of the street, narrowly missing a passing buggy.

Fargo stifled a chuckle and asked, with as straight

a face as he could muster, "Say, that stud's rank! You all right, kid?"

The boy stood up, shaking his limbs and checking for damage, and shouted, "Reckon so. I just don't know what's got into old Sunny."

"Thought you said his name was Charlie," Fargo replied.

"Sunny Charlie," the boy said, covering quickly. He dusted his britches off. "My ma named him." He said those four words as if they explained everything, and Fargo nodded.

The boy came back over to the Ovaro and stood there a moment, just looking at him. If he'd made a move to hurt the horse in any way, shape, or form, Fargo was ready to jump on him and pound him into the ground. For now, though, he was just willing to wait and see.

But the kid only patted the Ovaro on his neck and gave him an admiring look. He whispered something to the horse that Fargo couldn't hear, and then he looped the stallion's reins over the hitching rail again. He had given up, it looked like.

"What's your name, kid?" Fargo asked casually as he slowly stood erect.

"Toby," the boy said. "And I ain't a kid. I'm fifteen. Almost sixteen."

Well, Fargo hadn't been off by much.

He said, "Fair enough, Toby. You gonna leave old, uh, Sunny Charlie just tied up? It's gettin' kind of hot out here." He glanced up at the sun, which was directly overhead.

Toby shrugged. "I guess my pa will have to come get him. He can be a stubborn cuss."

Fargo grinned. "Your pa or your horse?"

Toby gave out sort of a lopsided grin. "Both?"

Fargo took a couple of steps forward, and stepped

down off the walk, right next to the Ovaro's head. "Well, Toby, you are one crackerjack of a fast thinker. And a good straight-faced liar."

Toby's face wadded up with indignation. "Hey! Who you callin' a liar, Mister?"

Fargo unwrapped the Ovaro's reins from the rail, then ducked under it, coming face-to-face with Toby.

"You, son," Fargo said conversationally.

Toby backed up a step, but backed right into the buckskin that was tied next to the Ovaro.

"Don't go runnin' off," Fargo said. Then he turned to the Ovaro and said, "Back."

The horse backed up until he was clear of the other mounts, then stopped, his head nodding, his reins dangling free.

Realization crossed Toby's face and stayed there, along with a good shot of panic. "Shit!" he muttered, and tried to duck under the buckskin's neck to make a break for it.

But Fargo was too fast for him. He grabbed the boy by his ragged shirt and hauled him back.

"Whoa up! Not so fast, there," he said. "How would you like a job, Toby?"

The boy's face went through a rapid series of changes, but finally settled on disbelief. "What?" he said. "You escape from some looney bin? You're crazier than I am!"

But Fargo just laughed at him. He did, indeed, have a little job for a boy who was quick in his mind and on his feet, and Toby had happened along at just the right time. He'd found the moose in the hen house, or so he hoped.

"Nope," Fargo said in all sincerity. "I'm not crazy, and I do have a job for you. If you can manage to be honest for a week. Just with me, though. The pay's two hundred and fifty bucks."

This time, Toby's eyes grew round as proverbial saucers. "You're connin' me, that's what you're doin'!" he said, but Fargo could tell there was something in him that wanted to believe.

"No con," Fargo said. "Now, you look like you haven't eaten in a week and a half. What do you say we take the Ovaro, here, down to the livery, and then I'll take you to lunch. My treat."

At this, the first mention of the Ovaro's name, Toby cocked his head. "The Ovaro?" He blinked a couple of times. "Hey, what's your name, Mister?"

"Fargo," came the answer. "Skye Fargo."

"Shit!" the boy yelped, and pulled one of those damned nickel books out of his back pocket. Fargo cringed. The boy unfolded it and excitedly pointed a finger at the figure on the cover.

"Hot damn!" he cried. "You're real? The beard, the bucks, the Ovaro. . . . I shoulda knowed you right off. Holy Hannah, the one and only Trailsman, right here in Dustin!"

"Better close your mouth before flies start layin' eggs in it, Toby," Fargo said, and started down the street. The big stallion, his reins still dangling, followed him like a giant black and white puppy dog.

Toby did much the same.

No other series has this much historical action!

THE TRAILSMAN

#244:	PACIFIC POLECOATS	0-451-20538-3
#245:	BLOODY BRAZOS	0-451-20553-7
#246:	TEXAS DEATH STORM	0-451-20572-3
#247:	SEVEN DEVILS SLAUGHTER	0-451-20590-1
#248:	SIX-GUN JUSTICE	0-451-20631-2
#249:	SILVER CITY SLAYER	0-451-20660-6
#250:	ARIZONA AMBUSH	0-451-20680-6
#251:	UTAH UPROAR	0-451-20697-5
#252:	KANSAS CITY SWINDLE	0-451-20729-7
#253:	DEAD MAN'S HAND	0-451-20744-0
#254:	NEBRASKA GUN RUNNERS	0-451-20762-9
#255:	MONTANA MADMEN	0-451-20774-2
#256:	HIGH COUNTRY HORROR	0-451-20805-6
#257:	COLORADO CUTTHROATS	0-451-20827-7
#258:	CASINO CARNAGE	0-451-20839-0
#259:	WYOMING WOLF PACK	0-451-20860-9
#260:	BLOOD WEDDING	0-451-20901-X
#261:	DESERT DEATH TRAP	0-451-20925-7
#262:	BADLAND BLOODBATH	0-451-20952-4
#263:	ARKANSAS ASSAULT	0-451-20966-4
#264:	SNAKE RIVER RUINS	0-451-20999-0
#265:	DAKOTA DEATH RATTLE	0-451-21000-X
#266:	SIX-GUN SCHOLAR	0-451-21001-8
#267:	CALIFORNIA CASUALTIES	0-451-21069-4
#268:	NEW MEXICO NYMPH	0-451-21137-5
#269:	DEVIL'S DEN	0-451-21154-5

**Available wherever books are sold, or
to order call: 1-800-788-6262**